TWO DOGS
IN A TRENCH COAT

Enter Stage Left

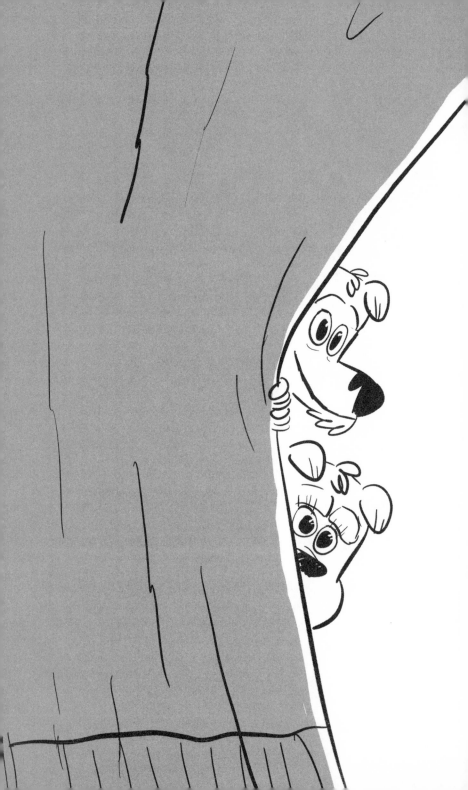

TWO DOGS
IN A TRENCH COAT

Enter Stage Left

by Julie Falatko

Illustrated by Colin Jack

Scholastic Press / New York

Copyright © 2020 by Julie Falatko
Illustrations copyright © 2020 by Scholastic Inc.

All rights reserved. Published by Scholastic Press, an imprint of Scholastic Inc., *Publishers since 1920.* SCHOLASTIC, SCHOLASTIC PRESS, and associated logos are trademarks and/or registered trademarks of Scholastic Inc.

The publisher does not have any control over and does not assume any responsibility for author or third-party websites or their content.

No part of this publication may be reproduced, stored in a retrieval system, or transmitted in any form or by any means, electronic, mechanical, photocopying, recording, or otherwise, without written permission of the publisher. For information regarding permission, write to Scholastic Inc., Attention: Permissions Department, 557 Broadway, New York, NY 10012.

This book is a work of fiction. Names, characters, places, and incidents are either the product of the author's imagination or are used fictitiously, and any resemblance to actual persons, living or dead, business establishments, events, or locales is entirely coincidental.

Library of Congress Cataloging-in-Publication Data available

ISBN 978-1-338-35899-5

10 9 8 7 6 5 4 3 2 1   19 20 21 22 23

Printed in the U.S.A.   23
First edition, January 2020

Book design by Elizabeth B. Parisi

To my acting teachers, James Collins and David Rowland, who never pretended to be furniture

CHAPTER ONE

Waldo could smell someone new in the room.
He turned his head and inhaled deeply. Yes.
He knew everyone's smell in the classroom, and there
was definitely a new human somewhere.

Waldo was doing what he always did on Tuesday afternoons, which was to sit on top of Sassy. Waldo was a small dog, and Sassy was a big dog, and every school day, Waldo rode around on top of Sassy, wearing a trench coat so they could pretend to be a student named Salty at Bea Arthur Memorial Elementary School and spend quality educational time with their boy, Stewart.

When they were pretending to be Salty, they did worksheets and sang songs and chased after baseballs.

They drew pictures and played with math cubes. And they got to experience the wonder and majesty of **school lunch**.

But Waldo could smell a new human in the class-room today, and it was confusing, because he could not see any new humans.

"Do you smell someone new?" he whispered to Sassy.

"Someone who smells like jazz shoes and hot lights?" said Sassy. "Yes."

Ms. Twohey, their teacher, clapped once, and then twice, and then three times. That was the special signal that everyone needed to be quiet and pay attention. Sassy and Waldo thought that it would be best if Ms. Twohey did her clapping and then gave everyone a **cookie**, but Ms. Twohey did not agree for some reason.

"Class, we have a special guest here today to tell us about— Oh! Where did he go?" Ms. Twohey started looking around, confused.

"Is the special guest imaginary?" asked Becky. "My little brother has an imaginary friend too."

"Our special guest is a real person," said Ms. Twohey.

"That's what my brother says too," said Becky.

Ms. Twohey opened the classroom door and stuck her head into the hallway. "Mr. Rollins? I wonder where he went." She came back into the classroom and looked helplessly at the students.

A man in a black turtleneck and black pants stood up slowly from behind Ms. Twohey's desk.

"Oh! There you are!" said Ms. Twohey.

"I was acting," said the man, "as your chair."

"Oh, the new smell is a human who is also a chair," said Waldo.

"He's not a chair," said Charlie. "He's the second-grade teacher. I saw him once when I was on composting duty and was gathering the second-grade **banana peels**."

"Children!" said the man, turning toward the class. "I am the second-grade teacher and also the drama teacher. My name is Mr. Rollins. I will teach you all to be actors."

Waldo raised his hand. "**What is an actor**?"

"An actor," said Mr. Rollins, "is someone who pretends to be something else, onstage, in a play."

"**I thought that was a liar**," said Waldo.

"No, they're different," said Mr. Rollins.

"**How**?" asked Waldo.

"Because everyone knows the actor is pretending, and still sometimes the actor does such a good job that the audience forgets for a bit. Like how I did such a good job acting as Ms. Twohey's chair earlier that no one noticed. When you don't know someone is pretending, that's a liar. Or a grifter. It's something very different."

"**Once, I saw a giant hot dog**," said Waldo. "**But it was actually a human on Halloween. Was that person an actor, a liar, a grifter, or delicious**?"

"Um," said Mr. Rollins.

"Are we going to watch you in a play?" asked Stewart.

"Even better," said Mr. Rollins. "You're going to be in a play!"

The class buzzed with excitement.

"Oh, hooray!" said Waldo. "I love to play!"

"You've been in a play before?" asked Susan.

"Playtime, yes," said Waldo. "It's my favorite."

"But they're talking about being in a play," said Stewart. "On a stage."

"There are many stages of play," said Waldo. "Before play, toy gathering, running in circles, napping."

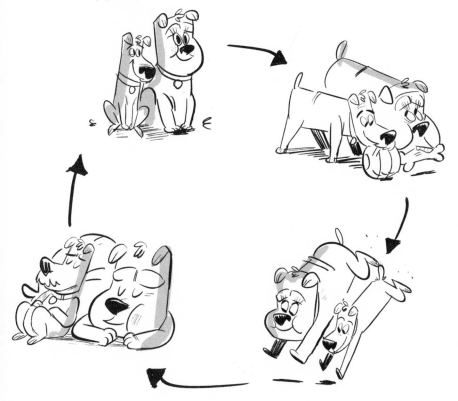

"No, like actors do," said Susan. "In a play."

"I don't like to play with liars," said Waldo.

Ms. Twohey tacked a sign-up sheet to the bulletin board.

"If you're interested in being in the play, you can sign up to audition here," said Ms. Twohey.

"I am going to sign up for play!" said Waldo, digging around in his desk for his favorite crayon. "That's fun."

Mr. Rollins started handing out a stack of booklets. "You should choose a monologue from this book for your audition piece," he said. "Choose something that gives you an opportunity to show off your range and depth."

"Range, like how far I can run when I'm playing?" said Waldo. "Depth, like how deep I can dig a hole?"

"Range and depth as an actor," said Mr. Rollins.

"When I play," said Waldo.

"*In* a play," said Mr. Rollins.

Salty and Stewart's friend Bax grabbed one of the booklets. "I hope there's something in here that'll really show off how awesome I am. I wonder if there's a speech that an action hero might give while he's hanging off the top floor of a skyscraper and about to jump onto a helicopter that's chasing him."

"I just want to pick a short one that'll be easy to memorize," said Stewart.

"You are going to be an actor?" asked Waldo nervously.

"I don't want Stewart to be a liar," whispered Sassy.

The dogs knew that Stewart liked to play, but they had never known he wanted to be in a play. Or pretend to be a chair. Or lie about being somebody else. Stewart was a good boy. He would never lie.

The class crowded around the sign-up sheet. Everyone wanted to audition.

"School is so many surprises," whispered Sassy. "We get to sign up for special playtime!"

Waldo wrote *SALTY* in big letters on the sign-up sheet.

"I am going to do the best at this new playtime," said Waldo. "And pretending to be a chair, if that's part of the playing."

"Don't forget that I am literally your chair all day long," said Sassy.

CHAPTER TWO

That night, Stewart set out to choose his mono-logue. There was one about being or not being, a few that were full of *thee* and *thou*, and one about whether or not you could handle the truth.

"This is going to be great," said Stewart, flipping through the pages of the book. "I wonder what part I'll get. It's going to be so fun to be in a play!"

"It is fun to play!" said Waldo.

Stewart had a feeling the dogs might not be getting it. "Well, it's not really playing. It's more like—"

"We love to play **Peanut Butter** Payback," said Sassy.

"Wait, what is that?" asked Stewart.

"It is **Peanut Butter** Payback," said Waldo. "You know."

"I really don't," said Stewart.

"We pretend we live in a world where **peanut butter** is the money," said Waldo.

"And all payments are in **peanut butter**," said Sassy.

"And we need to pay someone back," said Waldo. "Because we borrowed money."

"**Peanut butter** money," said Sassy. "So then we use our special skills to open the cabinet."

"What?" said Stewart.

"And blah, blah, blah we take the **peanut butter**, never mind, it doesn't matter," said Waldo. "You were saying something about this new playtime we're all going to do at school?"

"Yeah," said Stewart. "The play will be the whole class, up on a stage, pretending to be other people, with a beginning, a middle, and an end. It's kind of like how you pretend to be Salty every day."

"We don't pretend to be Salty," said Waldo. "We *are* Salty."

"I want to play," said Sassy. "On a stage with everyone."

"If you want to be in the play, you have to try out for it," said Stewart. "I'm going to pick one of the speeches from this book. You should choose one also. Then we'll perform the speeches for Mr. Rollins."

Sassy and Waldo read through the audition booklet, finally deciding on a passionate monologue about the importance of properly baked **sponge cake**.

Stewart chose a short speech where he was supposed to be the tortoise from the fable about the tortoise and the hare.

"I . . . am . . . the winner?" said Stewart, glancing at the booklet between every word.

"Why are you talking so slowly?" asked Sassy.

"I am having trouble remembering the words," said Stewart.

"Is remembering the words important?" asked Sassy.

"You should just read the lines!" said Waldo. "I

know you can read. I see you do it every day at school and even at night when you're in bed and Sassy and I are turning in circles to stamp down the imaginary grass in our beds like we are wild dogs."

"You know how you pretend to be wild dogs sometimes?" said Stewart. "Being in a play is kind of like that."

"But we are wild dogs," said Sassy.

"If you were wild dogs, you wouldn't refuse to go outside when it's raining," said Stewart.

"You are wrong," said Waldo. "If wild dogs knew how dry and warm it was inside, they'd stay in when it's raining too. But okay. We are wild dogs on the inside."

"Inside of the house," said Sassy.

"Inside of the house and inside of ourselves," said

Waldo. "We think like wild dogs, so then we become wild dogs."

"That's pretty much what acting is," said Stewart. "Doing that, and then memorizing your character's lines."

Both dogs lay down on the rug for a minute. They had to think. This was the first time Stewart had needed to memorize lines. Sometimes in class, they would read parts of a book out loud or read the stories they wrote. But they never had to memorize them.

"You are the best boy, both as regular Stewart and wild Stewart," said Waldo. "So I'm sure you'll be able to remember your lines no problem."

"Maybe if I practice more? I'm going to try to do the speech. Tell me if I forget a line."

Sassy and Waldo helped Stewart work on his lines. It didn't go very well. Stewart was having trouble remembering more than three words at a time. The dogs were as enthusiastic as they could be. But if one of the requirements for being in a play was to remember your speech, things were looking grim.

"I . . . will . . . treat . . . that . . . bunny," said Stewart. "Wait, is that it?"

"So close," said Sassy. "It's supposed to be 'I will beat the bunny.'"

"I have an idea," said Waldo. "We will do this the same way we trained you to give us treats. Every time you say the words in the speech right, you get a **Mister Barksy Crispy Chewie Sausage Snack**."

"I'm not sure that will work. And also that was me training you to sit and stay," said Stewart.

"I don't think so," said Sassy. "We already knew how to sit and stay. But we had to teach you to give us a treat when we did it."

"How about you take a break and I will practice our speech?" said Waldo.

Waldo read over the **sponge cake** speech. He was supposed to pretend to be a professional baker who was judging a baking competition. He knew it wouldn't be hard to pretend to be someone who cared about **food**. True, he didn't really care too much about **food** being baked or cooked or prepared in some specific special way. He just liked **food**. If it was undercooked, fine. If it was burned, sure. But he could understand how the **food** judge might care. Because although he didn't care if the **food** was burned to a crisp, he did care about **food**. A lot.

Stewart held the audition book, and Waldo stood authoritatively and pretended to be an important **food** judge.

"The thing about **sponge cake** is that it is not a kitchen sponge, Nanette! I thought you should know this by now. When you entered this competition, you knew it would be difficult. You knew there would be tears, and frustration. Baking is not a joke, Nanette! Baking is LIFE. And if you're going to make a **cake**, a **sponge cake**, you'd better make the best **sponge cake** you can, because if you don't, you're not taking it seriously. Which means you're not taking LIFE seriously. Can you do it, Nanette? I think you can. I want you to go back into the kitchen and do it all over. Bake a new **sponge cake**. Bake a **cake** that is perfectly golden, light, and airy. None of this dense, dry nonsense. You came here to bake a **cake**, Nanette. So bake one!"

Stewart looked down at the speech. "You got it all right," he said. "You didn't miss a single word! How did you even do that?"

"I think he is just good at remembering things related to **food**," said Sassy.

"Speaking of **food**," said Waldo, "let's go have another after-school **snack**."

"I need to practice my speech some more," said Stewart. "The audition will be a disaster if I can't remember these tortoise lines."

"Stewart doesn't want to have another **snack**?" said Waldo. "This playtime must be a very serious thing!"

CHAPTER THREE

Stewart wasn't getting any better at remembering his speech, but the dogs were sure they could help him memorize it.

"Stewart still smells nervous," said Sassy as she settled under their desk the next morning at school. "Even though we worked with him on his monologue for nine hundred hours yesterday."

"It is just because he is so excited about playtime," said Waldo. "Maybe tonight we should play **Peanut Butter** Payback with him. Then he'd remember his speech for sure!"

"Also **Peanut Butter** Payback will go much more smoothly if we have someone with thumbs to take the lid off the **peanut butter** jar," said Sassy.

"Anyway, Stewart will remember his speech in time," said Waldo. "The auditions aren't until after **lunch**. He can rememberize it by then."

"Also maybe **lunch** will help," said Sassy.

"**Lunch** always helps," said Waldo. "Also I am excited to do our own audition! Since after auditions we will have a lot of play!"

At the desk next to them, Stewart held the audition book in his lap. He looked up at the ceiling and mouthed the words of his speech.

"Wow, Stewart, you sure are sweating a lot for it being nine o'clock in the morning," said Waldo.

"Yeah, I know," said Stewart. "I can barely remember any of this speech. It's like the only thing I can remember is that the word *bunny* is in there, but I can never remember what the other words are or what order they come in."

"Maybe you should just say the word *bunny* over and over," said Sassy, "with feeling."

"Yes!" said Waldo. "Mr. Rollins will still see what a good player you are, even if you are just repeating one word! That's how great you are."

"You're supposed to say the whole speech though," said Stewart. "Not just one word over and over."

"Maybe the speech is the problem," said Waldo. "Because I am sure you are not the problem."

"Oh! That's it!" said Sassy. "You just need to pick a different speech!"

"I can't pick a different speech *now*," said Stewart. "Auditions are this afternoon!"

A noise across the room interrupted Stewart. "Ta-da!" Mr. Rollins unfolded himself from where he'd curled up on the puzzle shelf.

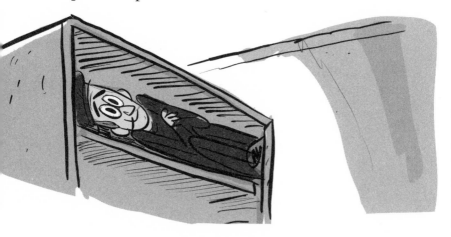

"Holy chalkboard erasers!" shouted Ms. Twohey. "How long have you been there?"

"I, Mr. Rollins, have been here but a moment, but I have been on that shelf, as a puzzle, for fifteen minutes. Today we will discuss what our play will be about."

"Yes, what will it be about?" asked Bax.

"That's the real question. And that," said Mr. Rollins, pausing dramatically, "is up to YOU."

"Up to me?" said Bax.

"Or any of you."

"What Mr. Rollins is trying to say is that you've been working so hard on your writing this year, so as a very exciting class assignment, you're going to write this play yourselves! And direct it too!" said Ms. Twohey.

"That is exciting!" said Waldo.

"Remember how we've been working on hooking your audience at the beginning? And having an exciting conclusion?" said Ms. Twohey.

"I do remember that, because I thought the best way to hook your audience would be with food, and the most exciting conclusion would be a big pile of food," said Waldo.

"Plus writing a script for a play will be a good opportunity for you to practice writing lots of dialogue," said Ms. Twohey.

"Is dialogue like a **nut log**?" asked Waldo. "I had one of those at Thanksgiving once."

"Dialogue is talking," said Ms. Twohey.

"I talked a lot about that **nut log**," said Waldo.

"Are you eating a **nut log** up there?" whispered Sassy. "Drop some down here."

"Everyone, take a deep breath," said Mr. Rollins.

"Why?" said Bax.

"We are going to practice being in a play where we are breathers," said Waldo.

"I took a breath in, and then I breathed out," said Piper. "Is that okay? Or do you want me to hold my breath?"

"You should definitely breathe out," said Becky. "I did, at least. Wait, can we breathe in again?"

"Listen to Mr. Rollins," said Charlie. "He's teaching us a special way to breathe. If you breathe in, and out, then in again, you're just breathing like you always do."

"Salty is breathing in and out very fast now," said Bax. Waldo was, in fact, panting. "I'm going to do that. That seems more fun."

Susan made a squeaking noise. Her face was very red. She exhaled noisily. "Why did you have us hold our breath?"

"I'm just trying to get you to relax," said Mr. Rollins.

"Try harder," said Bax, nearly out of breath.

Mr. Rollins led the class in a slow-breathing exercise where they were supposed to enter a state of deep relaxation so they'd be more creative. Deep breathing somehow made everyone less relaxed. They were all worried about whether or not they were breathing right.

"Now that you're all relaxed," said Ms. Twohey, "I want you to take out a sheet of paper and write down all the ideas you can think of for what our play should be about."

"Let your mind be free!" said Mr. Rollins. "Write down every idea, no matter how outlandish! We can make it happen!"

"Well, if they're too outlandish, they'll be hard to pull off," said Ms. Twohey.

"Nonsense," said Mr. Rollins. "We can pull off anything we set our minds to."

The class got to work writing down their ideas. They were excited. No one had ever asked them to write a play that they would also star in and perform for the entire school and also for their parents and probably some aunts and uncles and grandparents.

Ralph had ideas about a show where they all got to talk about how much they knew.

Bax had one idea involving spaceships, one that needed six army tanks, and one that required him to drive a race car around the stage.

"I have a good idea for a play," whispered Sassy.

"What is it?" Waldo whispered back.

"There are **meatballs** all over the stage," said Sassy.

"Is that it? Is that the whole idea?"

"Yes," said Sassy.

"That is a great idea. I will write it down," said Waldo.

Stewart came up with a lot of ideas for plays with no words so he wouldn't have to worry about memorizing his lines. Or maybe a play where they all read from books.

"My play is going to be one hundred percent beef!" said Waldo.

"My best idea is a kind of mime-in-the-library situation," said Stewart.

"I already wrote a play," said Arden.

"No, you didn't," said Bax. "Your idea sheet is still blank."

"That's right," said Arden. "I didn't write anything on this idea sheet, because I have a whole journal full of ideas at home. I love writing. I want to be a professional writer when I grow up. Or a dog trainer. Or a professional writer who has a lot of dogs. And maybe a goat. Anyway, I already wrote a play. It's at home. We should just use that."

Bax raised his hand.

"Yes, Bax?" said Ms. Twohey.

"I vote we use Arden's play. It's already written. I don't know if it has any race cars in it, but I'm sure we could add those in later. The important part is that I have a starring role. And then I won't have to write a whole play. Because Arden already did."

"Is that true, Arden?" asked Ms. Twohey.

"Yes!" said Arden. "It's called *The Wizard of Dogz*."

"Technically, that title sounds too much like *The Wizard of Oz*," said Ralph.

"It's called fanfiction," said Arden. "It's a type of writing where you take an existing story and rewrite it so most of the characters are dogs. At least that's the way I do it."

"So we all pretend to be dogs?" said Waldo. "Wild on the inside dogs?"

"Yes," said Arden. "I know a lot about dogs. I can help you if you want."

"I think I will be okay," said Waldo.

CHAPTER FOUR

I am so into this!" announced Bax as they walked into the cafeteria. "I am going to rock the audition! And the play! I can't wait to get up on that stage and sing my heart out!"

"Wait, there's singing?" asked Stewart.

"Oh, yes, definitely," said Arden. "It's not a play unless there's singing."

"Well, technically, that's a musical," said Ralph, checking the menu written on a whiteboard near the **lunch** window. "One **walking taco**, please."

"WHAT IS A **WALKING TACO**?" said Waldo.

"I take this **snack**-size bag of **Chipitos** and rip it open, and you get to choose **taco toppings**," said the **lunch** lady.

"My family always makes it when we're camping," said Charlie. "You can eat it from the bag and walk around the campsite. It's good. You'll like it."

"It is chips," said Waldo.

"Yes," said the **lunch** lady.

"And then **beef** and **tomatoes** and **lettuce** and **cheese**," said Waldo.

"That's right," said the **lunch** lady.

"And I am only learning about this **food** masterpiece right now?" said Waldo.

"It sounds like a **meal** you'd make up," said Stewart.

"I am sure it is something I have dreamed about," said Waldo. "I would like fifteen **walking tacos**, and you can put them on the ground so they can walk next to me to the table."

"Some of them will walk into my mouth," said Sassy.

"One **walking taco**, coming up," said the **lunch** lady. "Do you want **meat**?"

"**Yes**," said Waldo. "**All the meat**."

"And some more for me," said Sassy.

"Do you want **cheese**?" asked the **lunch** lady.

"**Yes**," said Waldo. "**All the cheese**."

"And some more for me," said Sassy.

"Do you want **lettuce** and **tomatoes**?" asked the **lunch** lady.

"**Yes**," said Waldo. "**Some of that**."

"And more **meat** and **cheese** for me," said Sassy.

Another **lunch** lady appeared in the window. "Good

choice, young child! Who's next, who's next? Step right up to the window of **lunch** wonder, and I'll get your order."

"Who are you?" asked the first **lunch** lady.

"I'm Minerva," said the new lady.

"Technically, you look exactly like Mr. Rollins," said Ralph.

"**You also smell like Mr. Rollins**," said Waldo.

"It is I, Mr. Rollins!" said Minerva, who was very clearly Mr. Rollins all along. "That's more acting! Method acting, which is when you really become the part. Fooled you all!"

"Technically, you didn't," said Ralph.

"You can't be back here!" said the **lunch** lady. "Shoo! Shoo! This area is for **lunch** workers only! No actors!"

Salty sat down at a table next to Stewart. Everyone was talking about the play.

Arden tried to explain what her play was about.

"So there's this group of friends," she said. "Dogothy, who is a dog. Rin-Tin-Tin Man, the Cowardly Leonberger, and Chewtoy, who is a giant dog toy who sometimes loses his stuffing and they have to stuff it back in. Dogothy and her little dog, Fofo—"

"The dog has a dog?" asked Ralph.

"**That happens sometimes**," said Waldo.

"Anyway, so Dogothy and Fofo are in Dogz, and they're trying to get back home. So Rin-Tin-Tin Man and the Cowardly Leonberger and Chewtoy take her on a quest to **Kibble** City to meet the Great and Powerful Wizard of Dogz, who is all-knowing and all-smelling and will be able to help them get back home."

"Is there a Wicked Witch?" asked Stewart.

"There is," said Arden hesitantly.

"A wicked witch?" Waldo whispered to Sassy. "That sounds scary."

"Is the witch a dog too?" asked Susan.

"Every person in the play is a dog," said Arden.

"Does the witch get water thrown on her and melt?" asked Charlie.

"No, but she gets wet and kind of smells bad," said Arden.

"Smells bad because the water was dirty?" asked Waldo.

"No, you know, because wet dogs smell gross," said Arden.

"I beg your pardon!" said Waldo.

"Does Dogothy get back home in the end?" asked Piper.

"Kind of. I'm still working on that part."

"You said this play was done!" said Ralph.

"It is," said Arden. "In my head. Most of it is written down. But there are some parts that I still need to actually, you know, put on paper."

"What kind of meals are in your **food**fiction?" asked Waldo.

"Fanfiction," said Arden. "There is **food** though. Rin-Tin-Tin Man carries a **kibble** can so he always has a **snack**, if he gets hungry."

"That is wise," whispered Sassy.

"Will they use real **food** in the play, or will that be lies too?" asked Waldo.

"Technically, it would be **dog food**," said Ralph.

"That would be delicious!" said Waldo.

"You're really getting into the part. You must be a method actor like Mr. Rollins was just talking about," said Ralph.

"The method of getting to eat delicious **food** while we play!" said Waldo.

"Don't forget about your legs down here when the **food** comes!" said Sassy.

"I'm going to train my amazing dog, Jeffy, to be Fofo," said Arden. "I wrote the part for him, and he is perfect. Plus he can fit into a basket and ride around and be adorable. He's so adorable."

"Do you think they'll let you bring a dog to school?" asked Becky.

"Of course they will!" said Waldo. "Dogs and school go together like **sausages** and **peanut butter!**"

"Jeffy is the best-behaved dog in the entire world," said Arden. "He'd be happy to sit in a basket and be carried around by whoever is playing Dogothy. Especially if we keep passing him **Happy Dog Brand Meat Crunchers.**"

"You should give those to all the actors," said Waldo. "To help. With acting."

"I can't wait to find out what part I get," said Bax. "I love acting. I'm the best actor."

"Have you memorized your audition speech?" asked Stewart nervously.

"Oh, yeah, totally," said Bax. "I memorized it in five minutes. It's easy. You just imagine you're the thing that's saying the words, and then, you know, easy, it's memorized."

"Oh, yeah," said Stewart. "Huh."

"Do not worry, Stewart," said Waldo. "I am sure you will have it memorized. You are doing such a good job!"

"Yeah, well, thanks," said Stewart. "Which speech are you doing, Bax?"

"I'm doing that song 'I Am the Very **Noodle** of a Modern **Lasagna Casserole**,'" said Bax.

"That song that won the world record for most words per minute?" asked Stewart.

"Yeah, sure," said Bax. "I like a challenge. What speech are you doing?"

"The tortoise and the hare."

Bax flipped through the audition book. "This one's only half a page."

"Stewart is so good that it only takes half a page for them to see how great he is at pretending to be a turtle boy," said Waldo.

"Cool," said Bax.

"I'm just so glad we're doing a play," said Piper. "It's going to be so fun! My cousin did a play about a frog at her school. They sang songs and dressed in costumes. She still sings the songs sometimes."

"My cousin learned a complicated dance for a play

he was in last year," said Charlie. "My grandpa still makes him do the dance every time we're all together."

"My cousin was in the commercial for Peter's **Pizza** Parlor," said Ralph.

"Wait, that's your cousin?" said Stewart. "In those commercials?"

"Yup," said Ralph.

"Peter's **pizza** is perfection!" said Stewart, Ralph, Becky, Piper, and Charlie.

"Wow, it must be good **pizza** for everyone to yell that out all of a sudden," said Waldo.

"That's the tagline from the commercials," said Ralph. "That's what my cousin says."

"Did he get a million dollars?" asked Bax.

"Nah, he didn't get any money," said Ralph. "They paid him in **pizza**."

"You can get PAID in PIZZA?" asked Waldo.

"Yeah, they gave him a lifetime supply of **pizza**," said Ralph. "Anytime he wants **pizza**, he can go into Peter's **Pizza** Parlor and get it for free. The funny thing is, my cousin used to be a Sally's Super **Slice** guy, but he doesn't ever go there anymore, since he gets free **pizza** at Peter's."

"So let me get all this straight," said Waldo. "Acting is when people know you are lying but you do it so well that they forget that while you play on a stage. And if you're doing it as a method, you have to become the thing you are lying about. Sometimes you get free **pizza** forever for acting. And acting is so much lying that you liked one **pizza** but then you get another **pizza** for free, so you don't like the old kind of **pizza** anymore in real life."

Just then the bell rang, and everyone started to line up to head back to class.

Stewart looked at the big curtain on one side of the room. "We'll be up there so soon," he said. "I'm so nervous about it."

"Why are we going to be on the windowsill of that giant window?" asked Waldo.

"What?" said Stewart. "What giant window?"

"I don't know about all of this acting," said Waldo.

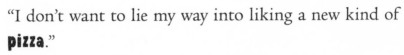

"I don't want to lie my way into liking a new kind of **pizza**."

"You both like every kind of **pizza**," said Stewart.

"Yes, but only because it's delicious," said Sassy.

CHAPTER FIVE

In a few minutes, after the custodians are done with **lunch** cleanup, we'll head back down to the auditorium for the auditions," said Ms. Twohey. "You'll all go onstage one by one to do your monologues."

"There's a stage in the auditorium?" said Waldo. "Where?"

"You know, on the end, where we line up when we're done with **lunch**. Where the big curtain is," said Stewart. The auditorium was also the cafeteria. And the gymnasium.

"Oh, I thought that was a huge window!" said Waldo. "I wondered why they never opened the curtains."

"You're funny," said Piper.

"Thank you," said Waldo.

"Stewart still smells nervous," whispered Sassy.

"Stewart, you are going to do so great as the tortoise boy in the audition," said Waldo. "Do not worry."

"Thanks," said Stewart, reading over his speech again. "I hope so."

Finally it was time. The class walked down to the auditorium and filed in to sit. The **lunch** tables had been folded and rolled away, like they were before gym class. A few rows of chairs had been set up where the audience would be. The curtains were open, and Waldo could see that what he thought was a window was actually a big stage for them to play on.

"Welcome, welcome to the theater!" said Mr. Rollins. "I am very much looking forward to hearing what you have brought to our space today. Remember, be quiet when you're not onstage, and clap for your classmates when they're done."

Bax went first.

"Now, Bax," said Mr. Rollins, "you can show everyone how it's done. When you come to the stage, I want you to say 'I, state your name, will be reading: title of speech.'"

"Sure thing, boss," said Bax, standing in the middle of the stage. "I, state your name, will be reading: title of speech. Also I'm doing the 'Modern **Lasagna Casserole**' song. And I'm Bax."

"You may begin," said Mr. Rollins, writing on a clipboard.

Bax did his song. He had also choreographed some fancy footwork to go with his singing. It was very impressive.

Bax finished and pumped his fists in the air. "Yeah!" he yelled. "Nailed it!"

"**Wow, you were really good**," said Waldo when Bax sat next to him.

"You remembered all your lines," said Stewart.

"Yeah, that's kind of the point," said Bax.

"Ugh, I know," said Stewart.

"Technically, the point is also to show how well we can embody the characters," said Ralph.

"Salty, you're up," said Arden.

Salty walked up the steps to the stage. Waldo felt prepared. He was excited to say his speech and pretend to be the baking show judge talking about **sponge cake**. And maybe he'd get free **pizza**, like Ralph's cousin. But he was also nervous. What if saying this speech made him into a liar? What if it convinced him to like another kind of **pizza**? What if he became somebody else and nobody noticed?

Sassy got to the center of the stage and sat. Waldo looked out at his friends in the class. They looked small. They were all staring at him. Mr. Rollins was writing something on the clipboard and then looked up at Waldo expectantly.

"Whenever you're ready," said Mr. Rollins.

Waldo knew it was time to start doing his **sponge cake** speech. Any moment now, he should start his speech. His first line was supposed to be "The thing about **sponge cake** is that it is not a kitchen sponge, Nanette!" He had practiced. He was ready.

But now, up high on this stage, staring out at everyone's faces, he didn't feel ready anymore. He felt thunderstruck. A light was shining in his face and was making him very hot. Sassy was also hot. He could tell because his paws, on her back, were getting hotter and hotter. Both Waldo and Sassy started to pant. Sassy's hot breath filled up the trench coat and made them both even hotter.

"I am going to melt," whispered Sassy. "You'd better do that speech soon, before all that's left of me is a puddle of dog."

"**Nanette**," Waldo squeaked. "**Sponges. Nanette.**"

After another long, awkward moment, Salty left the stage, returning to the row of folding chairs with a sigh.

"What happened up there?" asked Bax.

"**It is scary! You did not tell me it would be so scary!**"

"Oh no," said Stewart. "I don't feel so great."

"Pull it together, buddy," said Bax. "It's your turn. Get on up there."

Stewart stood, reluctantly. Waldo could smell that Stewart was a weird kind of beyond nervous that made him calm yet sweaty.

Stewart made his way to the center of the stage. He took a big breath.

"Whenever you're ready," said Mr. Rollins.

"I . . . may . . . be . . . a tortoise, but I will . . . beat . . . the bunny," said Stewart.

"He is saying it so slowly," whispered Sassy.

"I think he did it that way so many times that it's the only way he can do it," Waldo whispered back.

Mr. Rollins was writing a lot on his clipboard. Stewart kept going, speaking slowly, getting most of the words right.

"I am . . . the winner," he finished.

Mr. Rollins started clapping. He hadn't clapped for anyone else. He clapped the whole time a beaming Stewart walked down the stairs and went back to his seat.

"Marvelous, just marvelous," said Mr. Rollins. "Did you all notice the way Stewart really embodied the essence of the tortoise? How he made the deliberate choice to speak very slowly? Excellent work."

"Um. Thank you," said Stewart.

"Stewart," whispered Waldo. "You are the winner!"

CHAPTER SIX

The next day, they entered their classroom to find Ms. Twohey on the carpet, using a marker on an enormous piece of paper.

"This play is a great time for us to talk about schedules, and scheduling, and how to organize your time,"

said Ms. Twohey. "Especially since we'll have to figure out a way to practice the play and plan everything, from the set to the songs to the program."

"My parents are big on schedules," said Stewart. "Especially ones with highlighters and artistic hand lettering and special sections marked off in washi tape."

"Those are all good organizational tools," said Ms. Twohey. "We're really going to have to buckle down. A play is a lot of work."

"I put on plays with my brother all the time," said Becky. "They're no big deal. We do skits in the living room."

"Technically, skits in the living room are different from plays on a stage," said Ralph.

"That's true," said Ms. Twohey. "That's what I mean. Your parents and relatives are going to come to this play and record the entire thing and take photos and those artifacts will be around forever, so we have to make this play as good as possible."

"A **play is forever?**" said Waldo. "**I thought it was just for a few weeks.**"

Ms. Twohey showed them all the calendar she'd been working on. They were to devote their mornings to schoolwork and their afternoons to the play. It was going to be a very intense time. They only had three weeks to write, memorize, and rehearse the entire play, as well as build the sets and learn how to act and sing.

"The first thing we'll need is a stack of sticky notes in different colors," said Stewart.

"We'll get those later," said Ms. Twohey. "Right now it's time to go meet Mr. Rollins in the auditorium to talk more about what it means to be an actor."

The class lined up and went down to the auditorium.

"I did not know a play is forever," said Waldo.

"I think what Ms. Twohey was trying to say was that we'll hold the memories of the play forever, and that our parents will have those videos on their phones at least until they upgrade," said Becky.

They got to the auditorium, but Mr. Rollins was nowhere to be found.

"I'm sure he'll be along shortly," said Ms. Twohey.

"Being an actor can make you shorter?" asked Waldo. "Stewart, are you going to be very small when all this is done?"

"If Stewart's small, he won't be able to reach the **dog treats** that are kept on top of the refrigerator out of our reach," whispered Sassy, distressed.

"How about I tell you all about some of the songs I'm working on for the play?" said Arden.

"Yes, that's a good idea," said Ms. Twohey.

Arden pulled some papers out of her backpack and spread them out on the floor. "Okay, hang on, I have a song list somewhere in here."

"Let me know if you want me to get you some organizational sticky notes too," said Stewart.

"No, I'm okay, here it is," said Arden. "So far, the songs are 'We're Dogz to See the **Kibble**,' 'Somewhere Over the Dog Park,' and 'Ding Dong, the **Meal** Is Ready.' I'm also working on some that are originals, like one about how great dogs are, and one about how smart dogs are, and one about how cute dogs are."

"Fantastic!" said Mr. Rollins, hopping out of a trash can.

"Holy refrain and choruses!" said Ms. Twohey. "Have you been there the whole time?"

"Just doing some acting work, as garbage," said Mr. Rollins.

"How many songs are there going to be, Arden?" asked Piper.

"I'm workshopping twenty of them," said Arden. "But we'll probably use fewer than that."

"We'll have space for TWO songs!" said Mr. Rollins. "Three including the opening number."

"It'll all be great," said Arden. "Trust me. I might even use a tambourine."

"I'm not sure we'd be able to hear a tambourine all the way in the back of this room," said Mr. Rollins. "Do you have an electric tambourine?"

"My friend Roscoe has an electric circulating water dish," said Waldo.

"Like for a dog?" said Becky.

"For drinking," said Waldo.

"So what we're going to do today," said Ms. Twohey, walking up the steps to the stage, "is explore the space around the stage so we can start to think about how we'll set everything up."

Mr. Rollins put his hands on the stage and tried to hop up. It took him a few tries. He finally boosted himself up and then flopped forward onto the stage, rolled

a bit, and stood up. "I know you all were up here for your auditions, but I'd like you to come up and picture what it will be like when you're performing for an audience. Imagine there are people out there. Imagine you are wowing them. You'll take that positive energy into each rehearsal."

"I always wow everyone," said Bax, hoisting himself onto the stage much more gracefully than Mr. Rollins had.

"You all should use the stairs," said Ms. Twohey. "For safety."

Everyone decided that what Ms. Twohey said didn't apply to them, since Bax had gotten on the stage his own way. Half of them climbed up onto the front. Some of them used a ramp that went up the other side of the stage and ended up backstage. A few did go up the stairs but did it by jumping up each one. Waldo and Sassy went up the ramp and down the ramp, up the stairs and down the stairs, and then leapt up onto the stage. School was always so fun.

Ms. Twohey sighed. "Are you all up here now?"

"Oooh, guess what I am!" said Mr. Rollins, rolling himself into a stage curtain hanging in the corner. "I'm a **burrito**!"

"Where's a **burrito**?" said Waldo.

"**Burritos**?" said Sassy. "Toss one down here. No, wait, toss five down here."

"Weren't we supposed to imagine we were in a play?" said Ralph.

"We did that. Now we're imagining we have **burritos**," said Waldo.

"It feels good to be up here," said Stewart. "I'm so excited about this."

"So this is the stage," said Mr. Rollins. "This is what the audience will see. But there are important things that happen behind the scenes too. Let me show you what we keep backstage."

They all followed Mr. Rollins to one side of the stage.

"This is stage right," he said.

"You said that was the stage, right," said Waldo.

"No, I mean, this side is called stage right."

"But it's the left side of the stage," said Susan.

"Not if you're facing the audience," said Mr. Rollins.

"There is so much stuff back here!" said Waldo, looking around in awe. "They should put all this fun stuff on the stage so when we have playtime the audience can see it too."

"Technically, the point is that they can't see it," said Ralph.

"So, some of you will be onstage during the play," said Mr. Rollins, "and some of you will be backstage. The students working the crew will do things like making sound effects, or getting props ready, or opening and closing the curtains."

"I want to play, but I also want to play in the curtains!" said Waldo, thinking of all the curtain **burritos**.

"It's kind of dusty back here," said Becky.

"It smells like years and years of dust and nervousness," said Waldo. "It's very interesting."

"What are all these buttons for?" asked Stewart, looking at a big black panel covered in buttons and switches.

"Those are the audio and lighting controls," said Mr. Rollins. "I'll show you. Stewart, why don't you step onto the stage?"

Stewart walked to the middle of the stage. Waldo and Sassy watched proudly. Their boy was being chosen to be the example actor!

Mr. Rollins pressed a button, and a spotlight shone down on Stewart. He pressed another button, and some pink lights turned on toward the back of the stage, shining onto a backdrop. It looked like a sunset.

"That's really cool," said Bax.

"I feel like the star!" said Stewart, smiling.

"Of course you're the star!" said Waldo.

"We'll find out tomorrow what parts everyone got," said Ms. Twohey.

"That's right," said Mr. Rollins. "Final decisions are being made tonight, and the cast list will be posted tomorrow morning. Then you'll all know what part you're going to be."

"Part of what?" said Waldo.

"Which part in the play," said Mr. Rollins.

"Like someone will jump rope and someone else will bounce a ball?" said Waldo. "I hope I get to do playtime with lots of tennis balls."

"There are tennis balls," said Arden. "I think. I haven't gotten to that part yet."

"I'm so nervous about it!" said Charlie.

"Soon, soon," said Mr. Rollins. "Don't worry. You'll find out who you will be tomorrow."

"But Charlie is Charlie," said Waldo.

"But he'll be someone else in the play," said Becky.

"Someone else?" asked Waldo.

"We'll all be someone else in the play," said Stewart, who had walked out of the spotlight to join the class. "That's how it works."

"Someone else?" said Waldo again. "In the play? Stewart, you will be someone else too?"

"I hope so! I hope I get a good part!"

"Our Stewart will not be Stewart anymore?" whispered Sassy.

"Ms. Twohey said a play is forever," Waldo whispered back. "Is Stewart going to be someone else for good?"

CHAPTER SEVEN

Stewart kept tapping his spoon nervously against his **cereal** bowl the next morning at **breakfast**.

"Are you making music?" asked Sassy.

"Should we start singing?" asked Waldo.

"Nah, I'm just thinking about today," said Stewart.

"And how you won't have more bowls of **cereal** today?" said Waldo.

"I'm worried about getting a part in the play," said Stewart.

"We are also worried about that," said Sassy.

"I'm sure you'll get a part," said Stewart.

"We are worried about you," said Waldo. "We don't want you to become someone else. We love you, Stewart."

"Aw, I love you both too."

"But we love you as STEWART," said Sassy.

"I'll still be Stewart! I'll always be me."

"Well, then that settles it!" said Waldo.

"I just hope my part doesn't have too many complicated lines," said Stewart. "I've got to figure out a better way to memorize them. What if Mr. Rollins thinks I can only do a character that talks really slowly? I'm going to do some more of those breathing exercises in the mirror."

"Oh, but I was hoping you could show us how to open the **peanut butter** jar—before we go to school," said Waldo.

"Not today. I need to go try this out." Stewart got up, leaving the dogs alone with their **breakfasts**.

"Who says 'not today' to **peanut butter**?" said Sassy. "Wouldn't Stewart always say yes to **peanut butter**?"

"Do you think he is becoming someone else?" asked Waldo.

"I don't know. Wait. Hang on." Sassy lay down on the floor and fell asleep.

"Sassy! Why are you napping?" Waldo put Sassy's ear in his mouth to wake her up.

"I was thinking. And napping. It's called think-napping, and everyone is doing it. And what I thinknapped is this: Stewart has never before showed us how to open the **peanut butter** jar. So maybe he is still himself."

"But we never asked him before. And he's never had to look in the mirror to breathe. Breathing was always something he could do on his own."

"What is happening to our Stewart?" asked Sassy. "And when will he let us eat **peanut butter** straight from the jar?"

Everyone at school played on the playground before the bell rang, but the students in Ms. Twohey's class paced nervously by the door, waiting. As soon as the bell rang, they ran inside to the auditorium door, where there was a large piece of poster board that said THE WIZARD OF DOGZ: CAST. All the students had to crowd around it to see if they got a part.

"I'm Dogothy! I'm Dogothy!" shouted Piper.
"Right on, I'm Rin-Tin-Tin Man," said Bax.

Charlie was Chewtoy, and Susan was the Cowardly Leonberger. Becky was the Good Dog Trainer Witch of the Left Part of the Stage. There were students who were evil flying tennis balls, and two students, Lacey and Isaac, who were assigned to be the Great and Powerful Wizard of Dogz.

Finally Stewart had worked his way through the crowd to the cast list. Outside the school, he had convinced himself that it would be fun to have any part in the play, but then he heard that five of his classmates were cast as tennis balls, and now he wasn't so sure about that.

He ran his finger along the list of names until he found his own name, and then followed the line across to see what part he got. Next to his name was THE WICKED DOG TRAINER WITCH OF THE RIGHT PART OF THE STAGE.

"Yes! Yes!" said Stewart. "I get to be the evil one!"

This alarmed the dogs.

"Sassy," said Waldo. "Is Stewart bad now?"

"How could he be? He's such a good boy," said Sassy.

"But he's the Wicked Dog Trainer. So not only is he going to be someone else, he's going to be evil too?" asked Waldo.

"I can't take this," said Sassy, getting wobbly underneath Waldo.

"Stewart, how can you be a wicked dog trainer witch?" said Waldo. "You are not wicked or a dog trainer."

"I trained you both!" said Stewart. "Kind of."

"Pretty sure we trained ourselves," said Waldo. "We watched a video once. It was easy."

"So cool! Do you have a good evil laugh?" Bax called out. "That'll be the best part. To be able to do an evil laugh."

"I don't know," said Stewart. "Let me try. MWAHAHAHAHAHA."

Sassy dropped to the floor and put her tail between her legs. Waldo started involuntarily whimpering.

"Our Stewart!" squeaked Sassy.

"**Stewart, you are scary!**" said Waldo.

"I know, right?" said Bax. "Awesome, dude!"

Stewart could see how scared his dogs were. "I'm still me, Salty. I'm still Stewart. Remember? It's all pretend."

"**You were so good at that laugh though,**" said Waldo.

"Thanks!" said Stewart, to Waldo's dismay.

"Technically, I have the best part," said Ralph.

"What'd you get?" asked Bax.

"I'm the director!" said Ralph.

"Oh!" said Waldo. "You are the one who gives us all **pizza**!"

"There's no **pizza**," said Ralph.

"Yes! You told us!" said Waldo. "You said the director of your cousin's commercial play gave away a LIFETIME of **pizza**! Hurray! For **pizza**!"

"Hey, what part did you get, Salty?" asked Bax.

"Oh, I forgot to look because I was so distracted by **pizza**!" said Waldo.

The dogs checked the cast list and saw their name, Salty, next to: CREW.

"Who is Crew?" asked Waldo. "I hope Crew is not evil. I hope Crew gets all the **food**."

"Crew means you do important backstage stuff," said Stewart. "Like pressing that button that turns the spotlight on."

"Oh, good! I don't need to become someone else!" said Waldo. "I will be good at crew! I like pressing buttons. Do you think I'll get a **slice** of **pizza** every time I press a button? I got this important button-pressing job because I wowed Mr. Rollins in my audition."

"No offense, but you flubbed your audition," said Bax.

"But apparently I was not auditioning to be on the stage, but behind the stage," said Waldo.

"Yes, that's right," said Mr. Rollins, who suddenly stood up from where he had been pretending to be a bookshelf of free books three feet away from them.

"Oh, golly!" said Susan. "You startled me."

"Just like a good bookshelf would!" said Mr. Rollins.

"Oh, hi!" said Waldo. "Thank you for making me the crew dog. I like pressing buttons and getting food rewards!"

"You're thinking so much about all the dogs in this play," said Ralph. "You really are a method actor. Pretending to be a dog."

"Tell him we're meatball actors who are hungry now," whispered Sassy. "We need to get started on that lifetime supply of pizza."

"I think I'm going to try that method acting thing," Stewart said. "It might help me learn my lines."

"There must be a better way for you to learn your lines than doing the scary thing where you become the character forever," said Waldo. "I don't like that."

CHAPTER EIGHT

That afternoon, everyone gathered by the stage for their very first play rehearsal.

"Yeah, I'm Rin-Tin-Tin Man," Bax was telling everyone. "Rin-Tin-Tin Man is pretty much the star of the show. The entire plot hinges on Rin-Tin-Tin Man."

"Is that true?" asked Ralph.

"It might be," said Arden.

Mr. Rollins walked in and handed the pile of scripts to Salty to hand out to everyone. The play was currently two pieces of paper stapled together. Everyone started talking about how short it was.

"Now, listen," said Mr. Rollins. "One time I was cast as a bowl of pasta in an experimental play in a barn in Massachusetts. That was also one that was being written while we rehearsed it. Sometimes that's the way a play goes, especially if the play is especially new and groundbreaking."

Arden beamed.

"So we'll rehearse what we can, and Arden will continue to add to the play as she is inspired to add more," said Mr. Rollins. "And, Arden, you should be inspired to write about ten more pages, at least."

"Got it," said Arden. "I'll make a note of that." She took out a pink pen and scribbled on the corner of a scrap of paper and shoved it into her backpack.

"We're going to start by doing a table read," said Mr. Rollins. "Although we don't have a table, since the lunch tables have already been put away for the day, so we're going to sit in a circle on the floor."

"That is confusing," said Waldo.

"My parents sent me in with first-day-of-rehearsal presents for everyone," said Stewart.

"Did they send in a director's chair?" asked Ralph. "I noticed that I don't have a director's chair yet."

"Or one of those clapperboards that you clack down when you say, 'Action!'" said Charlie.

"Technically, those are only for movies and TV shows, although I would like to have one," said Ralph.

"Another thing we need is food," said Waldo. "Did your parents send you in with sandwiches?"

"I have highlighters!" said Stewart as he walked around and let everyone choose a highlighter. "So you can highlight your lines in the script."

The students sat in a circle and highlighted their lines.

"Let's jump right in," said Mr. Rollins. "Everyone ready? We'll start by reading our lines out loud."

Everyone started talking at once.

"Now let's do them one at a time, in order," said Ralph.

"That makes more sense," said Bax.

Piper, playing Dogothy, had the first line.

"Oh, what a boring life I lead," said Piper. Then she paused and looked at Ralph.

"You have the next line too," said Ralph.

"You said to do one at a time," said Piper.

"Let's just all read the script in order, one person at a time, and whoever has the next line can say it," said Ralph. "And also I know this is the first day, but I think it'll be good if everyone tries to get into character as much as possible while they're saying their lines."

"Uh-oh, they're getting into a character for this," Waldo whispered to Sassy.

"If only something interesting would happen," Piper continued as Dogothy.

Then it was Stewart's turn to say his lines.

"Mwahahahaha!" said Stewart. "I'll get you, Dogothy, and all your friends! I control the **kibble**, and I control all dogs! You can't run from me! I can see you in my magical **water** bowl! Mwahahahaha!"

"**Stewart!**" said Waldo.

"Yes, that was great, but let's try not to interrupt after every line, or this will take forever," said Ralph.

"Although that would be a way to make the play last longer," said Bax.

"**That was so scary**," said Waldo.

"Yeah, Wicked Dog Trainer Witch Stew, that was awesome!" said Bax.

"Keep going," said Ralph to Stewart.

Stewart pretended to look into his magical **water** bowl. "Oh, running that way, are you, Dogothy?" he said in his most evil voice. "I'll send my flying tennis balls after you! You'll never get away from me!"

Waldo whimpered involuntarily. Stewart patted him on the shoulder and whispered, "It's okay," and then smiled, a real, nice Stewart smile.

"Stewart is Stewart again," whispered Waldo. "But he was so good at being the Wicked Dog Trainer too."

"That's just what we were afraid of," said Sassy. "The transformation has started."

"I wonder if there's anything we can do to stop it," Waldo whispered back. "We have to save our Stewart from becoming evil."

CHAPTER NINE

That was awesome!" said Stewart on the way home.
"I love being in a play."

"There doesn't seem to be as much playing as I thought," said Sassy.

Waldo was walking a few steps behind them, trying to figure out if he was walking with Stewart or the Wicked Dog Trainer Witch who wanted to stop Dogothy from following the Yellow Snow Road. On the one paw, he smelled like Stewart. But on the other paw, there was an excited and proud smell that was different from other times Stewart had been excited and proud. When he had won the spelling bee in first grade, he had smelled happy and relieved. Now he smelled like he was full of joyous anticipation. And that could only mean two things: either they were having **hamburgers** for **dinner**, or he was very happy to be turning into an evil witch.

"I'm still pretty worried about remembering all my lines," said Stewart.

Stewart sure sounded like himself. Maybe Waldo was being silly. He trotted up next to Stewart.

"Before the play, we should spend the day recording everyone saying their lines, and then we'll play that during the performance," said Waldo. "The humans can move their mouths, and it will look like they are talking."

"Good idea. That way Stewart won't have to say those scary things himself, and he won't become the Wicked Witch forever," Sassy whispered to Waldo.

"I'm going to run through my lines so far right now while we're walking," said Stewart.

They stopped for a moment on the sidewalk so he could get out the script.

"What if the only way I can memorize them is by saying them really slowly, like I did for my tortoise speech? Although, maybe talking slow like that actually helped me get into that character? Hmm, I'm going to try something."

Stewart hunched over. He squinted and puckered his mouth. He lifted his shoulders up and wiggled his fingers.

"I'll get you, Dogothy, and all your friends! I control the **kibble**, and I control all dogs! You can't run from me! I can see you in my magical water bowl!" said Stewart.

Waldo stopped in his tracks. That was not Stewart. That was a witch who controlled all dogs.

"This is actually going okay," said Stewart. "It's not as hard to remember the lines if I try to think like a witch."

Sassy and Waldo exchanged worried looks.

"I think this will be a good way to memorize everything I need to," said Stewart, smiling.

And just like that, their Stewart, good Stewart, was back now. And even though he seemed nervous about remembering his lines, he also smelled so cheerful.

"I hope Arden doesn't add too many more lines. What if she adds a monologue and I have to talk for a long time? What if she adds two monologues?"

Sassy thought about all the actors she knew, trying to figure out how to help Stewart.

"What about Sergeant Barkles?" she said. "Sergeant Barkles never forgets her lines. Also she is such a good dog." Sergeant Barkles was a dog who was a real-life war hero, and then also starred in a lot of movies about her life. She was a great actor. Obviously.

"First of all, Sergeant Barkles doesn't have any lines," said Stewart. "All she does is bark."

"Those are her lines!" said Waldo.

"I guess," said Stewart.

Stewart looked over the script. It wasn't very long (yet), and he didn't have many lines (yet), and he was worried about what would happen as the play got longer and more complicated. He wanted so much to be the best Wicked Witch anyone had ever seen. It sounded so fun, to get up on the stage and pretend to be someone totally different from his normal self. And if he had to work day and night to memorize his lines, that would be fine. Probably.

"This play is going to be great," said Stewart.

"As long as we get that lifetime supply of **pizza**," said Sassy.

"I don't think we're getting any **pizza**," said Stewart.

"Ralph said!" said Sassy. "And a lifetime supply is a lifetime supply."

"Do you think we get extra **pizza** for the life we had before the play?" asked Waldo.

"Yes!" said Sassy.

"Do you think we get seven times as much **pizza** because every dog year is really seven human years?" asked Waldo.

"There's no **pizza**!" said Stewart.

This sounded just like something an evil dog trainer would say.

Stewart unlatched the gate into their backyard, and the dogs ran in circles for a few minutes. Stewart went inside to get them an after-school **snack**.

"Sassy, I'm worried about Stewart," said Waldo. "He says he's still Stewart, but he's also sometimes the witch."

"I know," said Sassy. "What if Stewart is so good at being the evil witch that he decides to be an evil witch forever?"

"We have to save him," said Waldo.

"How?" said Sassy.

"I have a plan," said Waldo.

"Okay," said Sassy. "What is it?"

"First we ask Ralph about that **pizza**," said Waldo. "When are we getting the **pizza**?"

"That is important," said Sassy. "But I don't see how that will save Stewart."

"Oh, that's a separate thing," said Waldo. "I just want to make sure we get **pizza**. We save Stewart by reminding him about all the great things there are in his life that he has by being Stewart."

"Like what?" Sassy asked.

"Well, like pencils. Does an evil witch use pencils and sticky notes?"

"Probably not," said Sassy.

"He likes not putting his laundry away too," said Waldo. "And everyone knows witches love putting away laundry."

"Also us. Witches don't have dogs; they have cats. If he becomes a witch, he'll have to get a cat."

"Exactly, and that is ridiculous," said Waldo.

CHAPTER TEN

oday instead of your regular art class, we're going to design the set for the play!" said Ms. Twohey. "Get out your drawing materials. Arden, tell us all the different places that are in the play so we'll know what we need to design scenery for."

"Well, there's Dogothy's house, before she goes to Dogz," said Arden. "There's the Yellow Snow Road, where Dogothy and Fofo meet all their new friends. There's the witch's castle, the field of mud where the witch sends her flying tennis balls to try to stop Dogothy, and then **Kibble** City, where they meet the wizard."

"This'll be easy!" said Bax. "We'll probably be able to build all this today. Do we have fifty sheets of plywood and a nail gun?"

"No," said Ms. Twohey.

"It might take longer than today, then," said Bax.

"Why don't we start with Dogothy's house?" said Ms. Twohey.

"I think it should be a big two-story house with a balcony," said Susan.

"I think it should be a doghouse," said Piper. "Since Dogothy is a dog."

"A **nice** **doghouse** **is** **one** **with** **a** **kitchen**," said Waldo.

"For **food**. Also carpeting. Sometimes not-carpeted floors are hard to walk on. For dogs. I've heard."

"Most doghouses don't have kitchens," said Susan.

"Sure they do," said Waldo. "And bedrooms and bathrooms and a living room with couches."

"That just sounds like a regular house," said Piper.

"That's what we're talking about," said Waldo.

"Sometimes it feels like these humans don't understand anything," said Sassy.

"Anyway, it'll technically be easier to build a doghouse than it will be to build a two-story house," said Ralph.

"Can the evil dog trainer witch's castle be really huge and awesome?" asked Stewart.

"Wait, what about the Good Dog Trainer Witch?" asked Becky. "Don't I get a castle?"

"No, there's no scene in the Good Dog Trainer's house," said Arden. "The Good Dog Trainer Witch just helps Dogothy get on the path to **Kibble** City."

"Well, I think you should rewrite it so I get a house," said Becky.

"If anything, we should rewrite it so every scene takes place on the same vast empty field," said Ralph. "Then we wouldn't have to build any sets and we could spend more time rehearsing."

"Maybe the Wicked Dog Trainer Witch should also live in a 'dog' house," said Waldo, doing quotation marks with his paws. "So he remembers just how much he loves dogs."

"Tell them that there should at least be portraits of cute dogs hung on the walls," whispered Sassy.

"The evil dog trainer witch *doesn't* love dogs," said Ralph. "That's why he's evil."

"But maybe he loves them just a little," said Waldo.

"Not really," said Arden.

"But maybe he loves dogs deep, deep down inside," said Waldo.

"I really think the Wicked Dog Trainer Witch should live in a scary Gothic castle," said Ralph. "Technically, that makes more sense."

"For the giant mud field, I think it's important to be authentic," said Bax. "We should absolutely bring in real mud."

"Yes!" said Waldo. "And puddles!"

"I love how you're letting your imaginations run free!" said Ms. Twohey. "But I don't think our principal, Ms. Barkenfoff, is going to approve of us spreading mud all over the stage. And remember that you'll be building everything yourselves, so make sure you don't design anything too elaborate or complicated."

"I think we should make an airplane that hangs from the ceiling on wires you can't see from the audience so Dogothy and her friends can fly to **Kibble** City," said Charlie.

"It would be cool if the Wicked Witch's castle had an elevator," said Susan.

"Do you think we can rig it so **Kibble** City emerges mechanically from beneath the stage?" said Piper. "That would be very dramatic."

"What should **Kibble** City look like?" said Stewart. "It's not going to be like the Emerald City in *The Wizard of Oz*."

"No, that would use too much glitter," said Arden. "What we need to do is build big skyscrapers to show how huge and beautiful **Kibble** City is, and all the buildings will be covered in fake fur."

"That's a great idea," said Susan.

"So we still need plywood and nails," said Bax. "Plus mud or, I guess, brown paper we can pretend is mud, although it won't be as real. And five hundred yards of fake fur. And paint. We're going to need a lot of paint."

Stewart was taking notes. "Do any of us know how to build anything like this? Does Mr. Rollins?"

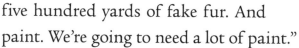

The map that was stored on one wall of the classroom suddenly unfurled, and Mr. Rollins fell to the floor.

"Hello, it is I, your local map, and also your local acting teacher, and local currently-out-of-work actor friend, here to answer your questions about building sets," said Mr. Rollins.

"Do you know how to build all this stuff?" asked Piper.

"I know how to do some light construction," said Mr. Rollins. "I'm also good at standing around eating **day-old pastries** while everyone else builds the sets. Which is good, since I'm supposed to take a largely supervisory role in this production."

"Luckily, we've been studying the principles of engineering," said Ms. Twohey, "so building these sets should be no problem."

"All we've built so far is a structure out of toothpicks and **marshmallows**," said Charlie.

"And our floats in the last Founders Day parade," said Arden.

"Right, but that was mainly gluing things to an existing float platform," said Piper.

"So we need to find an existing doghouse, an existing castle, and an existing skyscraper, and then we can glue things to them," said Bax. "No problem."

CHAPTER ELEVEN

I have a hammer!" said Waldo the next day at school.

"Well, hammer in the morning! And in the evening!" said Bax. "Point is, we have a lot of hammering to do to get this set built. All we've done so far is build the roof of the doghouse and glue a lot of brown fuzzy pretend fur to a big flat piece of wood."

"I want to hammer **meatballs** into one million smaller **meatballs!**" said Waldo.

"Then spill all of them down here!" said Sassy.

Sassy realized she had mistakenly stepped on a sticky scrap of fake fur, and she sat down to try to chew it off her paw and wait for the **mini-meatballs** Waldo had promised.

"Class, it's time to go down to the auditorium," said Ms. Twohey.

"Are we going to hammer there too?" asked Waldo as they walked down the hall.

"We're going to work on our lines, songs, and character motivation," said Ralph, setting his director's notes on the edge of the stage. "We were supposed to meet Mr. Rollins here, but I don't see him."

"I guess we should just have a **snack,** then?" said Waldo.

One of the folded-up **lunch** tables along one wall started to roll to the center of the room.

"What's happening?" said Susan.

"It's probably an earthquake or maybe a new dimension is opening and the floor is tilting," said Bax. "No big deal."

"It is I!" said Mr. Rollins, leaping out from behind the **lunch** table. "Your teacher! And a **lunch** table!"

"How come you're always pretending to be furniture?" asked Piper.

"I think it's more of a challenge to embody the spirit of an inanimate object," said Mr. Rollins. "Though some other members of my Thursday-night acting troupe claim it's just my shtick."

"You have a stick?" asked Waldo. "Can we all get sticks?"

"How come everyone but me has a stick?" said Sassy.

"Technically, a *shtick* means a gimmick," said Ralph. "Not a stick."

"A stick can be a gimmick," said Waldo solemnly, "if it comes from a gimmick tree."

"Today we should work on blocking," said Mr. Rollins.

"Blocks of cheese?!" Waldo shouted.

"Now you have cheese blocks up there?" whispered Sassy. "Give me one!"

"Technically, blocking

means how we move around on the stage," said Ralph.

"I wish one of these things was a **snack**," said Waldo.

Ralph jumped up onto the stage and consulted his clipboard. "It's very important that you remember your blocking. It helps so you don't all run into each other."

"**Running is fun!**" said Waldo.

"Like for this scene, Stewart, you stand here," said Ralph, pointing to a spot on the stage.

Stewart climbed onto the stage.

"You say your line, and then walk to here," said Ralph.

"Okay," said Stewart. "Oh, wait, I want to get into character first."

Stewart took a deep breath. He raised his hands and gnarled his fingers. He scrunched his nose and frowned. He bent over a bit and hunched his shoulders up to his ears.

"Oh no," said Waldo. "Come on, we've got to stop this." He gave Sassy a nudge, and she walked up the stairs to the stage, cowering.

"Dogothy thinks she's such a good dog," said Stewart in his evil witch voice, "but I'll show her."

Stewart started to walk across the stage. Salty ran over to stand in his way.

"Salty, what are you doing?" said Ralph.

"I am blocking," said Waldo. "Like you said."

"It doesn't mean physically blocking someone," said Ralph.

"Oh, silly me," said Waldo.

"Keep going," said Ralph to Stewart. "After your next line, you're going to start to move to the back of the stage to go back into your evil witch castle."

"I have a plan!" said Stewart the witch. He took three steps back. Salty stepped out from backstage and blocked him.

"Salty! I told you that you don't have to actually block him!" said Ralph.

"I am pretending to be the witch castle," said Waldo. "That is why I am standing right here and stopping him from going any farther or being any more witchy."

"We need to get through this rehearsal!" said Ralph.

"I will stop you, Dogothy!" said Stewart in his most evil voice yet.

"No!" said Waldo. "I will stop YOU, evil witch Stewart!" The dogs stood in front of Stewart.

"It's okay, you two," whispered Stewart. "You have to stop getting in the way. If you don't let us have rehearsal, we'll be here forever and then your **dinner** will be late."

"Oh," said Waldo.

"That would be tragic," said Sassy.

"We don't want you to be a witch," said Waldo.

"I'm still me," said Stewart. "Would I be talking to you about **dinner** if I was a witch?"

"I guess not," said Waldo.

"Talk to us about **dinner** some more," said Sassy.

"Technically, we're all just standing around now," said Ralph.

"We're ready to keep going," said Stewart. He turned toward his dogs and said in a quiet voice, "Remember **dinner**!" and then, before their eyes, transformed into the witch again.

CHAPTER TWELVE

L et's go to the dog park," said Stewart that after-noon. "It's such a nice day."

"Taking us to the dog park is something our good boy would do," said Sassy as they sniffed the sidewalk.

"Unless the wicked dog trainer wants to go to the dog park to train all the other dogs to be evil!" said Waldo.

Waldo and Sassy both looked at Stewart. He seemed like their regular good boy.

Stewart opened the gate, and the dogs ran in to greet their friends.

"Hi!" said Buttercup, a sprightly terrier. "What's wrong? You smell worried."

"We are afraid Stewart is becoming a wicked dog trainer witch," said Waldo.

"Every day he is acting a little bit more evil," said Sassy.

"Wow! Wow! Wow!" said Pistachio, yappingly. "That is a surprise! Your Stewart seems so nice! Wow!"

"Once my person tried to be a dog trainer for an afternoon," said Tugboat, a big gray dog with fluffy ears. "But she wasn't wicked. She talked in a Very Stern Voice, but I could tell she didn't mean it. At the end of the day, I got a **hamburger**. Is that what's happening for you?"

"No, we haven't gotten even one **hamburger**," said Sassy. "It's a totally different situation."

"Stewart is a wicked witch in a play, and the scary thing is, it seems like he does mean it," said Waldo. "When he's a pretender in the play, he is very good at it."

"Our boy is very good at everything, it's true," said Sassy.

"But he is also loving being bad," said Waldo.

"That's so very, very, very, very, very, very, very confusing!" said Pistachio.

"You should give him a **hamburger**," said Tugboat.

"You should give *me* a **hamburger**," said Buttercup.

"Me! Me! Me!" said Pistachio. "Give a **burger** to me!"

A scruffy small dog joined them. It was Arden's dog, Jeffy. "What are you all talking about?"

"Hi, Jeffy!" said Buttercup.

"We're talking about **hamburgers**," said Tugboat.

"**Hamburgers** and how Sassy and Waldo's boy is evil now," said Buttercup.

"What?" said Jeffy. "That's not true. I just saw him. He scratched my head! He smells totally not evil."

"It is because of the play your Arden is writing," said Sassy.

"Stewart is so excited about it that the part he's playing is taking over his life," said Waldo.

"I am in that play!" said Jeffy.

"Oh my gosh, oh my gosh, oh my gosh!" said Pistachio. "Are you evil too?"

"I get to ride around in a basket and eat **treats**!" said Jeffy. "It's going to be fun."

"See?" said Tugboat. "Jeffy is getting **treats**. You *should* give your human a **hamburger**, like I said. **Treats** protect against evil."

The dogs all nodded. This was so true.

"Time to go!" yelled Stewart.

"Thank you to our very good dog park friends," said Waldo. "We will protect our boy with **treats**."

CHAPTER THIRTEEN

Sassy and Waldo wanted to solve their problem when they got home from the dog park by giving Stewart a **hamburger**, but they had trouble, since they didn't have any **hamburgers**. Also Sassy admitted that if they did have **hamburgers**, she would be forced to eat them. For research.

"Today we need to work on writing the play," said Ms. Twohey the next day at school. "You all are working so hard on so many aspects of this production, but we're still lacking a complete script."

"I don't know why the whole class has to help me write the play," said Arden. "I've got it under control."

Arden shuffled through the pile of papers on her desk. Some of them fell on the floor. Arden picked them up and tried to put everything in order. Papers were sideways and upside down. Some of the papers were ripped half pages or words written on the backs of envelopes.

"Do you not like regular pieces of paper?" asked Waldo, helping her pick up the pages.

"I've been working on it as inspiration hits," said Arden. "And sometimes I can't find a good piece of paper to write on when that happens."

Waldo picked up a box of **cereal**. "You wrote your play on **Flaky Flakes**? I will tell you something, and this is from me, someone who loves **food**. I admire you using **food** as paper, but also **food** is not paper."

"Hey, I'm hungry too," whispered Sassy. "Pass a few scenes down here."

"No, I wrote on the box," said Arden, showing Waldo all the writing on the back. "It was the only thing I could find one morning while I was having **breakfast**."

"**What did you do with the Flaky Flakes**?" asked Waldo.

"I put them in a big bowl and then they got stale. I gave some to my dog, Jeffy, but my mom told me dogs shouldn't eat too many **Flaky Flakes**. So then I ended up making them into **Peanut Butter Chocolate Flake Balls**."

"This is such a good story," said Waldo, drooling a little. "No wonder you are the play-writing person."

"All I want to know is how many lines the Wicked Dog Trainer has," said Stewart.

"Dude, this is a MESS," said Bax, looking over Arden's pile of papers, boxes, and envelopes.

"Actually, a lot of history's great writers were disorganized slobs," said Ralph.

"Gee, thanks," said Arden.

"This is wonderful, Arden," said Ms. Twohey. "I can

see that you're working hard and have a lot of ideas. And while I, personally, am a lot more organized than this, you need to do whatever method works for you."

"I think we should let Arden keep working so the rest of us can hammer more nails," said Bax. "I really like hammering those nails."

"One thing you could do is not make the evil dog trainer witch so mean," said Waldo.

"Technically, that makes no sense," said Ralph.

"We also need to design the program," said Ms. Twohey.

"Once, I had **program crackers** with **peanut butter** on them and they were delicious," said Waldo.

"No, not **graham crackers**—programs," said Stewart. "A program is a little paper booklet that lets the audience know who is in the play."

"If you put the **peanut butter** on the right way, you could make the **crackers** into a little booklet," said Waldo.

"I'm down here waiting for some of those **peanut butter crackers**," whispered Sassy. "Pass them down."

"Can I do it and draw things on it?" asked Charlie. "I like drawing."

"I love hand lettering," said Becky. "Can I write everyone's names in it?"

"I love eating," said Waldo. "Can I eat all the **crackers** after you write all over them?"

CHAPTER FOURTEEN

Good thing we have fixed the play! Everything is going great. We built most of the set and glued fur to things," announced Bax as they all walked into the auditorium that afternoon after school.

Arden walked in, carrying a folder stuffed with scraps of paper, as well as a detailed list outlining what order the scenes should be in.

"Hey, where's Mr. Rollins?" asked Stewart.

"He's probably hiding behind that table," said Bax.

"Or he's under that blanket," said Becky.

"Any minute now, he's going to jump out from behind something," said Arden.

"Yep, any minute now," said Bax.

"We can get started without him, right?" asked Stewart.

"You bet we can," said Bax. "We're a self-governing collective."

"Technically, we're just a group of kids putting on a play, but since I am the director, we can start," said Ralph. "Even though I still don't have a director's chair."

"Or **pizza**," said Waldo.

"Is there **pizza**?" whispered Sassy.

"All right, everyone, let's start where we left off yesterday," said Ralph. "Dogothy has been swept by the wind to this new place, and everything seems strange to her and Fofo. The Good Dog Trainer Witch of the Left Part of the Stage has just told Dogothy that the way for her to get back home is to find the Wonderful Wizard of Dogz. Becky, you say your line that starts 'All you need to do is' and we'll go from there."

"All you need to do is follow the Yellow Snow Road," said Becky. "And that will take you to **Kibble** City.

I am going to give you these magical ruby sneakers, which belonged to the Terrible Dog Groomer from Way Over There."

"They're beautiful!" said Piper. "Plus they look like sensible shoes for going on a long walking journey. Thanks! Bye!"

Piper skipped from one side of the stage to the other.

"It's time for Chewtoy," said Stewart, looking over the paper scraps that served as the script.

"Charlie, you're up!" said Ralph.

"Now, you're a discarded chew toy," said Arden, looking over what she had written. "You should kind of wad yourself up, like a dog chewed on you for a while and then forgot about you."

"That's so silly!" whispered Sassy, laughing. "What dog would forget about a chew toy that they had already chewed on for a while? That means it was a good one! And remembered forever!"

"If Charlie is a discarded chew toy, then it means he was not a good one, and not chewed on," said Waldo.

"What?" said Charlie. "I'm a good one!"

"But if you are good to chew on, you would not be discarded," said Waldo.

"Look, I don't think it matters," said Ralph. "Let's say you're beloved. All that matters right now is you're on the side of the Yellow Snow Road, and Dogothy finds you."

"Okay, I can work with that," said Charlie. "As long as I know what my motivation is. I really want to become this character."

"You know," said Waldo, "it is not necessarily important to become the character. Everyone could also just say their lines and still be their own selves."

"It's kind of the point to have us all become the characters," said Becky.

Just then Mr. Rollins ran through the door, panting. "Sorry I'm late!" he said. "I gave my class a math quiz AND a vocabulary quiz."

"You are such a good teacher!" said Waldo. "Staying late to give your class so many quizzes and then also being our acting teacher."

"No, the quizzes were this morning," said Mr. Rollins. "I'm late because I fell asleep on the couch in the teachers' lounge."

"Well, luckily we were rehearsing just fine without you," said Ralph. "Our only issue was deciding whether the character of Chewtoy should be benevolent and beloved, or disgraced and discarded."

"Oh, definitely disgraced and discarded," said Mr. Rollins. "That's much more interesting. There can be a whole song about how far you've fallen, and how you'll never be good again."

"My mom is not going to like that at all," said Charlie.

"All right, from the top, everyone!" shouted Mr. Rollins, tapping a stick on the back of a chair. "A-five, six, seven, eight!"

Waldo sidled up next to him. **"Maybe you do not know,"** said Waldo. **"But counting starts with 'one.'"**

"We've already done it from the top," said Piper. "Why do we have to start again?"

"You're right! That's all we have time for today because I was so late," said Mr. Rollins, looking at his watch. "Great job, everyone. I think we're off to a good start. Keep up the same level of dedication that you showed today, and we're going to have a great show. It'll be intense and you'll have to focus, but it'll be worth it. Remember, you can relax at the cast party!"

"What's a cast party?" asked Waldo.

"It's the gathering we'll have when it's all over, after the play is all done. It's a nice way to celebrate before our lives go back to normal," said Mr. Rollins.

"So our lives and our Stewart will go back to normal," whispered Sassy. "At this *cast* party."

"We can do it," said Waldo. "We can save our Stewart!"

"There's something else very important," said Sassy. "Will there be **food** at the cast party?"

CHAPTER FIFTEEN

The next day Mr. Rollins was not late to rehearsal. It started right on time, even though Sassy and Waldo were hoping it wouldn't. They had even gone so far as to make a **kibble**wish the night before, which was when they wished on a **kibble** before they ate it (it was very hard to do, because they had to wait an extra three seconds to make the wish before eating). Even a **kibble**wish did not stop the rehearsal.

"Let's warm up before today's rehearsal with an improv exercise," said Mr. Rollins. "Okay, we're going to need four emotions, six professions, some blindfolds, and a bucket of dialogue lines."

"**Hungry!**" shouted Waldo.

"What?" said Mr. Rollins.

"**That's an emotion**," said Waldo.

"Technically, exasperated!" said Ralph. "We're all warmed up! There are barely any days left until the performance! We don't have time for improv!"

"There's always time for improv," said Mr. Rollins.

"**Still hungry!**" said Waldo.

"Salty, I've loaded all the sound effects into the sound board," said Mr. Rollins. "Let me show you how it works."

"Yes, okay," said Waldo. "Is this the part where I get to press a button?"

"Yes," said Mr. Rollins.

"How come you did not pop out from behind a garbage can or from inside the **burrito** stand that is hidden in the curtain?" asked Waldo.

"Because right now I am acting as a crew member."

"Just like me!" said Waldo.

Mr. Rollins led Salty backstage. The rest of the class continued to rehearse the play onstage.

"I like how I can see the side of everyone from here," said Waldo. "There is a couch! And a box of clothes!"

"Let's go over to the couch and take a nap," said Sassy.

"Can the actors see me?" asked Waldo.

"Well, if they turn to the side, sure, they can see you," said Mr. Rollins.

"Because it feels like this is an invisible room," said Waldo. "Can the audience see me?"

"No, the audience won't see you," said Mr. Rollins. "That's what makes your job backstage seem like magic. The sound and lighting effects you do will just seem to happen from the audience's perspective. If you're doing it right, they won't know you're back here."

"We will get to do a good job and nobody will know it's us, like how we keep all the squirrels from coming into the house and making the bathtub into their poolside resort," Sassy whispered to Waldo.

"But don't worry, your name will be in the program so they'll know that you are working on the crew, even if they don't see you," said Mr. Rollins. "They'll know you pressed the button to make the sound of thunder, even if they choose to believe that thunderclap is real and happened on its own."

"Oh! It's Stewart! Hi, Stewart!" said Waldo.

Stewart, who had just come up onstage to do his part, laughed and waved at Salty.

"You're not supposed to distract the actors," said Mr. Rollins.

"But that is Stewart," said Waldo. "He's my best friend."

"That's even more reason not to distract him," said Mr. Rollins. "Don't you want him to stay in character?"

"No!" said Waldo. "I do not! I want him to stay in Stewart!"

"How about I show you the control boards now?"

Waldo was awed by all the buttons on the sound and lighting boards. There were buttons and knobs and sliders. Some things were labeled, but unhelpfully. The important thing was that it all looked like a lot of fun to play with.

"I've got it from here!" said Waldo.

"I haven't showed you how any of this works," said Mr. Rollins.

"I will figure it out!" said Waldo.

"Slide one of those control boards down here so I can play too," said Sassy.

Waldo started to shove the lighting board off the table it was on.

"What are you doing?" asked Mr. Rollins.

"Putting this on the ground," said Waldo.

"Why?" said Mr. Rollins.

"So I can use my feet. And also my hands. I will control both at once. This is a lot of jobs, doing both sounds and lights, and it only makes sense to work the lights with my feet."

"No, you can do it all with your hands, I promise," said Mr. Rollins. "It's not that hard."

"That wouldn't be fair though."

"Wouldn't be fair for who?"

"For . . . my feet."

"Let me show you how it works, and then you can decide later if you think it's necessary to multitask."

Waldo was pretty sure he could figure out how the sound board and lighting board worked without Mr. Rollins's help. Or, well, he knew he didn't know how it worked, but he'd been standing there wanting to press all the buttons for several minutes and had wasted time trying to give the lighting board to Sassy, and Stewart was still onstage, and now was clearly the time to start pressing buttons.

So he did.

Waldo started with one small button, and a tiny corner near the back of the stage lit up blue. See? Easy. Waldo pressed three more buttons, and spotlights shone on the stage. Stewart was now standing in darkness and stepped into one of the beams of light.

"You think you can run from me, Dogothy!" said Stewart. "But I will find you! Mwahahahaha!"

Waldo quickly pressed those buttons again so Stewart wasn't standing in a spotlight anymore. Stewart couldn't be evil if he didn't have a light to stand in.

Waldo slid some switches up, and the back of the stage lit up orange. Then he pressed a button on the sound board and a loud *cock-a-doodle-do!* came from a speaker behind him.

"Stop pressing all the buttons," said Mr. Rollins.

"Yes, I will keep pressing all the buttons," said Waldo in a button-pressing daze. "That is a good idea."

Waldo slid both paws over as many buttons as he could on the sound board. There was the sound of rain, wind, a siren, a horn honking, a phone ringing, and a cow.

"Cut!" yelled Ralph from the audience. "What's going on back there?"

Salty stepped onto the stage. "Oh, hello," said Waldo. "I am the button presser."

"That's enough buttons for now," said Ralph. "It's kind of hard to get our lines right when you've got a bunch of barnyard animals on a city street happening back there."

CHAPTER SIXTEEN

Waldo and Sassy sat on the floor of Stewart's room a few days later, watching him nervously. He was reading over some new lines Arden had written. Was he turning into the Wicked Witch? He still seemed like Stewart. He still smelled like Stewart.

"Mwahahahaha!" said Stewart, practicing.

"Oh no," said Waldo.

"It's happening," said Sassy.

"Quick, get a **hamburger**!" said Waldo.

"If I could get a **hamburger** every time you yelled 'Quick, get a **hamburger**,' then we would have a lot of **hamburgers** right now," said Sassy.

"What are you talking about?" asked Stewart.

"How are you?" asked Sassy.

"What? I'm fine," said Stewart.

"Who are you?" asked Waldo.

"What's with you two?" asked Stewart.

"You are very good at doing the playtime," said Sassy.

"Too good," said Waldo.

"I know Mr. Rollins said we just have to make it to the **food** party, but Ms. Twohey said a play is forever," said Sassy.

"And since we haven't been able to find any extra **food** to give you as protective **treats**, we are worried you are going to keep some of the witch parts in you even when the curtain closes," said Waldo.

"We did find some protective **treats** on the counter, but we ate those," said Sassy.

"Is that what you're worried about?" asked Stewart. "I only need to be the evil witch for a little while. I thought I explained that."

"See, that's very confusing," said Waldo. "You are not going to become the witch but you are going to become the witch? I am worried you are going to be confused and forget when you are supposed to be evil and when you're not."

"And then you'll be the Wicked Witch at Stewart times," said Sassy.

"And feed us sand for **dinner**," said Waldo.

"That is a terrible thing the Wicked Witch would do," said Sassy.

"I'm not going to feed you sand!" said Stewart. "I promise. In fact, it's **dinner**time now. Let's go downstairs and I'll feed you the **Gravy Bites** you always get."

"No sand?"

"No sand."

"Hey there, kiddo," said Stewart's dad in the kitchen. "How's that play coming along? I heard you've done a lot of good work highlighting your lines!"

"Let us know if you need any help!" said Stewart's mom.

"Oh! I forgot!" said Stewart, putting the dogs' bowls of **kibble** down on the floor for them. "I need a costume."

"A COSTUME?" said Stewart's dad.

"A WHOLE COSTUME?" said Stewart's mom.

"Yeah. By tomorrow. Sorry about that," said Stewart.

"Don't apologize!" said Stewart's dad.

"I'll be right back!" said Stewart's mom, running out of the kitchen.

She came back a minute later wheeling in two large boxes.

"Okay, I got our emergency craft kit and our emergency sewing kit," she said. "Now, tell us all about your costume."

"Well, as you know, I'm the Wicked Dog Trainer Witch," said Stewart. "So I need a wicked cloak and a wicked hat."

"So much wicked," said Waldo.

"Got it," said Stewart's dad. He pulled out some purple velvet. "We can make the cloak with this."

"They had a sale last week at the sequin warehouse, so I've got plenty of spangles," said Stewart's mom. "Do you want purple or black?"

"Uh, both?" said Stewart.

"Innovative," said Stewart's dad, threading a needle. "Oh! Where are the hat-making supplies?"

"Here they are!" said Stewart's mom. She pulled out a cloth tape measure and wrapped it around Stewart's head. "You're such a good boy, surprising us with a craft project like this."

"I am going to make a LIST," said Stewart's dad.

"Good thinking!" said Stewart's mom.

"Hat, brim, cloak, sequins," said Stewart's dad, writing each item in a different color pen.

"Do you want your cloak to have sleeves, or should it be more of a cape?" asked Stewart's mom.

"And do you want the sequins to be in the shape of something, or a random scattering, like stars?" asked Stewart's dad.

"Whatever you want," said Stewart. "It doesn't really matter."

"That's hilarious!" said Stewart's mom.

"Of course it matters!" said Stewart's dad.

"It matters a great deal!" said Stewart's mom.

"Well, sure," said Stewart. "I just meant it doesn't matter to me, because I know whatever you decide will be great."

Stewart's mom put her hands over her heart. "Our boy. So good."

"How did we get so lucky?" said Stewart's dad.

"Now go! Leave us! We've got work to do!" said Stewart's mom.

Stewart and the dogs walked back to his room.

"Stewart's parents sure seem to think he is good," said Waldo.

"They are going to have an unpleasant surprise when they find out he plans on becoming evil," said Sassy.

"They are going to help him, and we should too," said Waldo. "He is our Stewart. No matter what. And it is our job to protect him and play with him and help him."

"When the curtain closes, it will all be over," said Sassy, yawning. "Then our Stewart will be Stewart forever again. So we just need to make sure the play ends. But now let's nap."

"We can't save Stewart without napping first," said Waldo.

Stewart picked up the new pages for the script and sat on his bed.

"Yeah, of course he's still Stewart," said Sassy. "How could our boy be anything but Stewart?"

Waldo yawned. "Even his parents say he's a good boy. We're being silly."

"Mwahahahahaha!" said Stewart.

CHAPTER SEVENTEEN

"Well, tonight's the night," said Ms. Twohey. "You've been working on this play for three weeks, and it's all coming together tonight."

"Tonight is not the play!" said Waldo. "It's the **salad dressing** rehearsal, where we are all worried that our human friends are going to turn into their characters forever. Although I still don't know why."

"A *dress* rehearsal is where we do the whole play from beginning to end as though we're putting it on for real," said Becky. "It's a trial run. It's called a dress rehearsal because we all wear our costumes."

"Technically, we might not be able to put it on from beginning to end, because there's no ending," said Ralph.

"I'm working on it!" said Arden, hunched over her desk, writing quickly.

Waldo looked at Arden, who was still writing the play even though they were supposed to perform it for everyone's parents and grandparents on Friday.

"Sassy, Arden is still writing the play," whispered Waldo.

"Is she still writing it all on regular paper?" asked Sassy. "If she starts writing on **food** again, pass some of the play down here to me."

"What if she doesn't finish writing it?" asked Waldo.

"The play needs to end. If it doesn't end, Stewart will never go back to normal."

"We need our boy back!" said Sassy.

Mr. Rollins came in wearing a black turtleneck and small glasses.

"You are not pretending to be a workbook or a piece of chalk!" said Waldo.

"I am acting as a director today," said Mr. Rollins, speaking in a British accent.

"Technically, I'm the director," said Ralph.

"I shall be the director's director," said Mr. Rollins.

"That's not a thing!" said Ralph.

"Remember, Mr. Rollins is only acting," said Ms. Twohey. "He's not really the director. Mr. Rollins, you are such a good actor, and I think you might be frightening Ralph."

"Oh, thank you, thank you," said Mr. Rollins.

"You're thanking her for scaring me?!" said Ralph.

"No, only for the part about me being a good actor," said Mr. Rollins. "Are you all ready for tonight? I'll see you in the auditorium at four p.m. sharp!"

The dress rehearsal was the first time everyone saw one anothers' costumes. Stewart wasn't sure how his parents finished his whole costume in one night—it was just the kind of thing they did. He tried not to think too much about it.

"Charlie! You look adorable!" said Piper.

Charlie, dressed as Chewtoy, was wearing a giant mangled costume.

"Charlie looks delicious," said Sassy.

"Check me out as Rin-Tin-Tin Man," said Bax, strutting. He had a big hat and long, floppy ears, as well as a satin bomber jacket. "I made this costume all by myself. WOW, look at you, Stewart!"

Everyone stopped to admire Stewart. His pointy hat was shiny and had spotted ears attached to it. The cloak fit him perfectly, even when he spun menacingly. Stewart kept scrunching his nose and frowning, looking very evil.

"Mwahahahaha!" said Stewart.

"Dude, super scary!" said Bax, putting his hand up for a high five.

"Now that Stewart has his costume on, he has forgotten how to be Stewart," said Sassy.

"Stewart!" shouted Waldo. "Remember how much you love pencils! And pencil sharpeners."

"I only love wicked witch things!" said Stewart, staying in character.

"What about dogs?" asked Sassy.

"YES! DOGS! Don't you love dogS?" said Waldo.

"My pets are all flying tennis balls!" said Stewart. "I am a wicked dog trainer who trains dogs to do whatever I need them to do to carry out my evil plans! Oh, hey, Jeffy."

Arden had just walked in with her dog, Jeffy, who would be playing the party of Dogothy's dog, Fofo.

"Hello to my good friend Jeffy!" said Waldo.

"How is it going with your good boy?" said Jeffy.

"We have had a sad lack of **hamburgers**," said Sassy. "So all we can do is keep reminding him of who he is, but it doesn't seem to be working."

"Good luck," said Jeffy. "And let me know if you find those **hamburgers**!"

Arden picked Jeffy up and handed him to Piper, who was dressed in a blue-and-white-checked dress. She also wore perky dog ears on a headband and had used makeup to paint a round dog nose on her regular nose.

"If anything happens to Jeffy, I'll never forgive you," said Arden.

"He'll be fine!" said Piper. "He's going to be great."

"Here is a bag of **Meat Crunchers**," said Arden. "You can tuck this into his basket. If you need him to do anything, you can bribe him with **Meat Crunchers**."

"Maybe we should all have some **Meat Crunchers**," said Waldo. "For authenticity."

"Piper, will you paint on my dog nose?" asked Susan.

"Do you want a **Meat Cruncher**?" asked Waldo.

"Ew, no thank you," said Susan.

Isaac walked by doing a series of squats and lunges.

"Is that your new walk?" asked Waldo.

"I'm strengthening my quads to be the lower half of the Wonderful Wizard of Dogz," said Isaac. "Will you help Lacey balance when she tries stacking on top of me?"

"Excuse me, what now?" asked Waldo.

"Lacey will be riding on my shoulders so we can be an extra-tall dog."

Sassy laughed from underneath Waldo.

Isaac braced himself. Lacey climbed onto a desk and then onto Isaac's shoulders.

"That's ridiculous," whispered Sassy.

"I know," said Waldo. "They're the size of five German shepherds. No dog is that big."

"She'll never stay up on him like that," said Sassy. "He needs to bend his knees for stability."

"It feels like you're going to fall off," said Isaac.

"This isn't as easy as I thought it would be," said Lacey.

"It never is," whispered Sassy. "It never is."

CHAPTER EIGHTEEN

$\mathcal{S}$alty stood backstage, ready. This was it. Or . . . almost it. It was the dress rehearsal, which was the pretend performance. And the whole performance was everyone pretending. Since that's what acting was. And sometimes Stewart pretended to be the witch even when the play wasn't happening. And there was still no ending, which meant Stewart could be stuck like this forever.

Plus they hadn't gotten any **pizza** yet. Or even any **Meat Crunchers**, which were right there, in Jeffy's basket.

Waldo watched while Piper fed Jeffy a **Meat Cruncher**. Waldo drooled a little.

Ralph was pacing nervously backstage, wearing a wireless headset and furrowing his brow. He kept checking a clipboard.

"Okay, two minutes until curtain," said Ralph.

"Are you talking to me or to someone else wearing a headset somewhere?" asked Waldo.

"Technically, both," said Ralph. "Are you ready?"

"Yes! I am going to press a button!"

"And open the curtain," said Ralph.

"What?" said Waldo. "Then all of the burritos will fall out."

"I am ready," said Sassy.

"Just get ready to open the curtain," said Ralph, pointing at some heavy ropes. "Right after you start the opening music in three, two, one . . ."

"What, now?" asked Waldo.

"Yes, now!" said Ralph.

Waldo pressed the button that he remembered was the one that started the music, and the sound of an orchestra playing a grand opening song came out of the speakers. The stage was dark, but Waldo could smell that Piper and Jeffy (and the bag of **Meat Crunchers**) were waiting on the stage next to the large wooden doghouse that the class had managed to build.

"We need to go to those giant ropes," said Waldo. "Somehow we are going to use those to open the curtain."

Sassy walked over to the ropes. Waldo tried to press them with his paw. He batted at them. Sassy carefully stuck her head out from under the trench coat and started chewing on one of the ropes. Sassy loved to chew on rope.

"I do not think we are supposed to eat it," said Waldo, but he also put some rope in his mouth, just to be sure.

Sometimes Sassy and Waldo played tug with a big braided toy that they had at home. It was very fun. And now, with this rope in both of their mouths, they remembered how fun it was.

"It's mine!" said Sassy around the rope in her mouth.

"No, it's mine!" said Waldo, pulling hard in the other direction.

Sassy was not one to give up easily, and as the bigger dog, she thought it was her duty to always win at

tug. So she pulled down on the rope, very hard. Then, to her surprise, the curtain started to open.

"More! Faster!" said Ralph. "What are you waiting for?"

"We're waiting to figure out how this thing works," whispered Sassy, pulling harder. They both pulled on the ropes until the curtain was open all the way.

Waldo pressed a button that lit up the stage, and Piper started saying her lines. Waldo felt very professional. Then Waldo leaned on the sound board, and a regal trumpet call blared out of the speaker.

"Oops," said Waldo, waving at Ralph, who was glaring at him.

Piper finished singing "Somewhere Over the Dog Park," and then Ralph said, "Okay, time to start the wind."

Waldo was supposed to press a button that made a howling wind noise, and then start a fan that would blow wind onto the stage. But he couldn't remember which button was the wind button. He kept staring at the board but couldn't find the right one. He guessed at three buttons, but they were the sounds of cheering, a duck quacking, and a car horn. Piper looked nervously offstage at Salty.

"Just start the fan," said Sassy.

Waldo turned the fan on HIGH, which blew Piper and Jeffy halfway across the stage.

"I can't remember which button to press for the sound!" said Waldo. "We will have to make the howling wind effect ourselves."

Waldo and Sassy didn't know how to sound like wind, but they did know how to howl, which they started doing. It made for a startlingly effective windstorm, especially since the fan was so strong it had started blowing Dogothy's doghouse to the other side of the stage.

"Fade to black!" said Ralph, and Waldo slid the button down on the light board that would make the stage dark so they could change the scene.

"Phew, glad that's over," said Waldo.

"Technically, that was only the first scene," said Ralph. "We still have the rest of the play to get through."

CHAPTER NINETEEN

School that Friday was a jumble. There were last-minute fixes on some costumes, and they had to nail in an extra stabilizing leg to the back of the huge skyscraper in **Kibble** City, which had been very wobbly during the dress rehearsal.

The rest of the dress rehearsal had been similarly wobbly. Everyone remembered most of their lines, although they had to make up the ending, since Arden hadn't written it yet. Waldo and Sassy remembered when they were supposed to change the scenery and when they were supposed to do most of the sound effects, and only plunged the stage into total darkness twice by mistake. And Stewart was terrifying. All in all, Ralph had called it "technically a disaster," which was not a full disaster.

But now it was opening night. Stewart helped Waldo and Sassy label all the buttons they needed on the sound and light boards, and he was so happy and helpful that the dogs were sure he had probably maybe remembered to not turn evil.

Susan was making a new courage medal that she would wear as the Cowardly Leonberger, after she decided the one she had worn in the dress rehearsal wasn't big enough. The new one was the size of a **dinner** plate.

Charlie and Becky finished drawing and lettering the programs and took them down to the office so the school secretary, Dottie, could copy them. Arden was going to hand out all the programs to people who came to see their play. Everyone gathered around when Charlie and Becky came back from the office.

"Oh, it looks so real!" said Arden. "Look! '*The Wizard of Dogz*, a new play, by Arden.' That's so cool!"

"I like right there where it says, 'Directed by Ralph,'" said Ralph.

"Let me see," said Waldo. "'Salty: Crew.' It's me! It's my name!"

"I want to see my name in it!" said Susan.

"Me too!" said Bax.

"Me too!" said Mr. Rollins, who had followed Becky and Charlie upstairs. "Look, there it is: 'Faculty Adviser: Mr. Rollins.'"

A small boy wandered into the room. "Mr. Rollins? We're done with our **snack**, and the student teacher is reading a book to herself."

"Thank you very much, Russ. Actors, I have to get back to my second graders. I will see all of you"—he paused dramatically—"TONIGHT." He twirled out of the room.

Arden was sitting in a corner of their classroom on the floor, surrounded by papers.

"Hello to my good friend Arden," said Waldo. "I am here to help you finish the play."

"Oh, thanks," said Arden distractedly. "I'm good. I don't need help."

"Maybe you do just a little though?" said Waldo. "I wrote it for you."

Waldo handed her some pieces of paper. Arden took the papers and squinted at them.

"This is a drawing of a **sandwich**," she said. "And what does this say? 'They were all very good dogs the end'?"

Waldo nodded proudly. "That's right."

"That's not really an ending," said Arden.

"Sure it is!" said Waldo. "You can use it. Just have someone say that, and show a picture of a **sandwich**, the end, play is over, everything is back to normal, cast party, we get Stewart back."

"What?"

"I am worried that there will be no ending," said Waldo.

"Yeah, you're maybe the hundredth person who has said that to me," said Arden. "It'll be fine. I'm almost done. But I can't finish if people keep coming over and asking me if it's done yet."

"I will leave now," said Waldo. "I will also draw more drawings of **sandwiches**. Just in case you need them."

CHAPTER TWENTY

That night, everyone gathered in the music room to get into their costumes. Mr. Rollins was jumping up and down giddily. Arden brought a stack of programs to the auditorium door. Sassy and Waldo were pacing. They weren't nervous about the show. They were worried about Stewart. If Stewart did a bad job with the play, he would be sad. If he did a good job, he might never stop being evil. It was a lot to deal with.

Plus they had to push all of the buttons and work the curtain. But if they got it all right, and the play ended, then they could get to the cast party, where there would maybe be **food**. And then hopefully, Stewart would be back.

A few minutes before the play began, the actors, Ralph, and Salty all went through a door in the hallway that led backstage.

"It's like a secret passage," said Susan.

"A secret passage to your destiny!" said Mr. Rollins.

"What?" said Bax.

"Assuming your destiny is to be an actor," said Mr. Rollins.

The sounds of talking and bustle started filtering in from the auditorium on the other side of the curtain. The students could hear excited anticipatory voices and the noise of metal folding chairs being inadvertently moved and scraped along the floor as their families found places to sit.

Mr. Rollins peeked out around the curtain.

"Lots of excitement out there. Looks like a great audience tonight."

"Technically, it's all our parents," said Ralph.

"We're on in three minutes," said Mr. Rollins. "I want you to bring the same enthusiasm that you've been bringing to rehearsals, everyone. If we're lucky, they'll book us for a few more weeks."

"It's a school play," said Arden.

"We have to go back to our regular school schedule on Monday," said Becky.

"Don't give up on your dream!" said Mr. Rollins. "Ready? Let's all gather in a circle. Now, let's all say this vocal warm-up exercise together: the lips, the teeth, the tip of the tongue."

"The lips, the teeth, the tip of the tongue," said everyone.

"The **chips**, the **beef**, they drip on my tongue," said Waldo.

"I'm going to go watch from the audience," said Mr. Rollins. "Break a leg, everyone!"

"**What**?" said Waldo. "**What is that supposed to mean**?"

"It's probably a **chicken leg**?" said Sassy. "Or maybe a **turkey leg**? Where do you think the plate of **turkey legs** is? I'm hungry."

"Me too," said Waldo. "**Excuse me, Ralph? Where are the turkey legs to break in my mouth with my teeth**?"

"And we're on in three, two, one, GO!" said Ralph, pointing at Waldo.

Waldo pressed the button labeled OPENING MUSIC, waited five seconds, and opened the curtains using both his paws and his teeth for extra speed, and the play had begun!

CHAPTER TWENTY-ONE

Waldo and Sassy were keeping an eye on Stewart. He hadn't gone on yet, but he looked terrifying in his costume, and he kept practicing his wicked face.

"So far, so good," said Ralph, standing nearby and studying his annotated script.

"Let us know if it becomes so far, so bad," said Waldo. "That's what I'm worried about."

Two women in the audience had elbowed their way to the front of the stage and were filming Piper and smiling proudly.

Everyone in the audience was holding a phone or camera or, in one case, a huge video camera like they use to record television shows, up above their heads.

"They are all making movies," said Waldo.

"I wonder if any of them are making **pizza** commercials?" asked Sassy.

Becky came onto the stage, and a new set of parents came forward, phones up in the air, with big, proud smiles on their faces. The people who were sitting in the front row had to lean to one side to see around the parents in front who were filming.

"Oof, this reminds me of when I used to go to Screaming Bakers shows back in the day," said Mr. Rollins, who was now backstage. "It smells like armpits down there."

"It smells like armpits from up here too," said Waldo. "And if you have any extra **steamy bacon**, I will eat it. I am very hungry."

"I'm going to go watch from the catwalk," said Mr. Rollins, pointing at the raised platform high above the stage that all the lights and scenery were attached to.

"Are there CATS?" asked Waldo.

"I'll be the cat," said Mr. Rollins, pretending to lick a paw.

"Is there a dogwalk?" asked Waldo.

"Not here," said Mr. Rollins, and he leapt, catlike, onto the scaffolding that led up above the stage and climbed to the top.

"What if Stewart stays the Wicked Witch forever, even after the play is over, because he gets a cat from the catwalk?" said Sassy.

"We'll keep all the cats away from him," said Waldo.

Stewart was onstage, looking into a bowl of water. It was supposed to be like a crystal ball that he could see things in, magically. He was watching Dogothy, Fofo, the Cowardly Leonberger, Rin-Tin-Tin Man, and Chewtoy as they were trying to work their way across the field of mud. They had not used real mud, even though Bax wanted to, but instead balled-up pieces of brown paper. It didn't look much like mud, but the parents filming it didn't seem to mind.

"You'll never make it across this magical field of mud!" said Stewart wickedly.

183

"Stewart! You are a good boy!" whispered Waldo loudly from the side of the stage. Stewart broke character for just a moment and smiled.

"I'm getting sleepy," said Susan as the Cowardly Leonberger, doing a big fake yawn.

"Let's lie down for a bit," said Charlie as Chewtoy.

"It's this mud!" said Piper. "This mud is making us tired! Quick, everyone, put on these booties! Then you won't get mud on your paws!"

Piper, as Dogothy, took felt boots out of her basket and handed them to everyone, who put them on and continued across the mud field to safety.

"This is very unrealistic," said Waldo. "Everyone knows that those booties take two

hours to put on. It's important to run away from them for an hour and then to stand very still once they are on."

"This play has a city made of dog fur and flying tennis ball minions, and that's the part you're focusing on as being unrealistic?" said Ralph.

"I just think it's important that the dog parts are right," said Waldo. "So it's believable. To the audience."

"We did it!" said Dogothy. "We made it across and now can finally go to **Kibble** City and get back home!"

Dogothy hugged her friends. Everyone in the audience said, "Awwwwww."

"Technically, they're not worried about realism either," said Ralph. "Get ready, it's almost time for the Great and Powerful Wizard of Dogz scene."

Isaac and Lacey were standing in the wings near Salty. Lacey had a dog mask on.

Waldo and Sassy had known that Isaac and Lacey were playing the Great and Powerful Wizard of Dogz, and they had watched Lacey climb onto Isaac's shoulders and fall off, but that was only the dress rehearsal version. This real version, in front of a full audience, looked extra silly.

Waldo and Sassy couldn't stop laughing.

"What's so funny, Salty?" asked Piper.

"Who's going to believe those two children are one huge dog?"

"Okay, get ready to switch scenes, Salty," said Ralph. "Cue the between-scene music, and . . . go!"

Waldo pressed a button and a jaunty tuba song started playing.

"Not that between-scene music!" said Ralph. "Never mind. Fade to black. And bring in **Kibble** City."

Salty ran onto the stage and gathered all the brown-paper mud balls. Then he and Ralph rolled the towering flat furry buildings that were the skyscrapers of **Kibble** City onto the stage before running back to the wings.

They saw Stewart waiting offstage.

Waldo whispered, "Remember how we have so much fun running around in the grass together!"

"Good thing you have us to give belly rubs to!" whispered Sassy. "You love doing that! Which is a thing good humans love!"

Stewart smiled.

Waldo faded out the music and brought up the lights, and Piper, Charlie, Susan, Bax, and Jeffy came back onstage.

"You're doing a great job," said Stewart to his dogs.

"A great job of being the crew?" said Waldo.

"Or a great job of making sure you stay Stewart forever?" said Sassy.

"There it is! **Kibble** City!" said Piper onstage. "Isn't it beautiful?"

"And there's the Great and Powerful Dogz!" said Bax. "Awesome!"

Isaac walked onto the stage with Lacey balanced on top of him. They had been practicing all day and had gotten much better at walking as one giant dog and not falling apart into two humans.

"I am the Great and Powerful Dogz!" said Lacey in a commanding voice. "I know why you've all come here. Dogothy, you want to go home. Cowardly Leonberger, you want a medal for your collar. Rin-Tin-Tin Man, you want new kibble. And, Chewtoy, you want a new squeaker. I'm pretty sure I'm going to get you all you asked for. I'm not sure. I need to take a nap first. At any rate, I'm not granting any wishes at all until you complete one task for me. And it's kind of a big one, to be honest. All you have to do is get the Very Special Good Dog Rewards Bin from the Wicked Dog Trainer Witch of the Right Part of the Stage."

Waldo pressed a button that made the sound of a dramatic thunderclap. The parents all laughed.

"Why did they laugh?" said Waldo. "It's supposed to be scary."

"They're parents," said Ralph. "Technically, parents don't make any sense."

Stewart was getting ready for his next big scene. He twirled around a few times in his wicked cloak and scrunched his eyebrows together.

"Don't forget that you love dogs," said Sassy.

"And paper clips," said Waldo.

"Fade to black!" said Ralph, and as Waldo was sliding the lights down to darkness, he watched in horror as Stewart's face changed from their lovable boy that was sweet and kind to the angry scowl of the Wicked Witch.

CHAPTER TWENTY-TWO

Onstage, Charlie, Piper, Susan, and Bax approached Stewart.

"Mwahahahaha!" said Stewart. "Sit! Stay!"

"The witch has put some sort of immobility spell on us!" said Becky.

"What are we going to do?" said Piper.

"We'll never get our wishes granted if we're just

stuck here ten feet away from that bin of Very Special Good Dog Rewards," said Charlie.

"Nobody gets my bin of Very Special Good Dog Reward **Treats**!" said Stewart. "Only very good dogs get those! And you are not very good dogs! STAY!"

"I'm scared!" said Piper.

Waldo and Sassy were also scared. Stewart had been the Wicked Witch more and more every day. And while everything was supposed to be back to normal when the play was over, they weren't so sure. Stewart was so good at being the Wicked Witch. What if he decided to be the witch forever, for fun, and to get cats instead of dogs and to laugh that horrible laugh all the time instead of his regular, nice Stewart laugh.

There was something else. Stewart smelled like he was having fun, but he also smelled like he couldn't remember his lines. He had only gotten the lines for this scene today, when Arden had finally finished writing the play. He had done his best to memorize them, but now, under the hot lights, they could tell he did not remember what he was supposed to say.

"We can't let Stewart forget his lines," said Waldo.

"Also we have to make sure the play ends," said Sassy.

"It's showtime."

They ran onto the stage.

"Dude, what are you doing?" said Bax.

"I am saving you!" said Waldo. He turned to Stewart. "And saving you too!"

"Awwwww!" said the audience.

Waldo picked up the bin of Very Special Good Dog Reward **Treats**.

"You are all good dogs," he said, handing the bin to Piper. "Each and every one of you. Dogothy, you are a very good dog. Your dog, Fofo, is also of course a very good dog. And now that I have given you this big bin of **treats**, I am just going to help myself to this bag of **Meat Crunchers** from Fofo's basket. Hi, Fofo, you are doing a great job. I'll take these **Meat Crunchers**, thank you. Even you, Wicked Dog Trainer Witch of the Right Part of the Stage. You might be evil, but down deep, you are a very good dog. You should stop being evil, and run around in the park and think about things. Being evil might seem like fun right now, but it is not fun!"

Waldo wasn't sure what else to do. He had said what he needed to say. Did they save Stewart? They would have to wait and find out. He walked offstage.

Piper pretended to throw the magical bowl of water onto Stewart.

"It smells like wet dog in here!" said Charlie.

Becky came on from stage left.

"You could have gone home any time you wanted, Dogothy," said Becky. "All you had to do was chase your tail three times and say, 'There's no **snack** like **bones**.'"

Piper spun around three times and said, "There's no **snack** like **bones**!"

Waldo shoved her doghouse onto the stage, and it rolled to a stop right by her feet.

"And there it is! Home!" said Piper.

"End the play!" said Ralph. Waldo and Sassy worked together to pull the curtain closed, and then there was the sound of thunderous applause.

"**We won!**" said Waldo.

Mr. Rollins had climbed down from the catwalk. "Time for the curtain call!"

"Curtain!" called Waldo.

"Go ahead," said Mr. Rollins.

"Curtain!" said Waldo again.

"What are you doing?" asked Mr. Rollins.

"I am calling the curtain," said Waldo. "Do you think if I call to it very nicely, it will spit out our burritos?"

"A curtain call is when you open the curtain and all the actors bow to the audience," said Mr. Rollins.

"Oh, why didn't you say that in the first place?" said Waldo, and he and Sassy opened the curtain.

Everyone bowed to their parents, who cheered and clapped. Then Arden came out, and they all cheered for her. Then Ralph came out, and they cheered for him. And then Salty came out, and as far as Waldo and Sassy could tell, the parents cheered the loudest for them, which was nice. They walked back offstage and closed the curtain, and it was all over.

"We made it," said Waldo. "It is finally all over."

"We have to go find Stewart," said Sassy.

They found Stewart in the music room, getting out of his costume.

"Stewart?" said Waldo. "Is it you?"

"Hi!" said Stewart.

"He smells like himself," said Sassy.

"You were so scary, Stewart," said Waldo.

"Thanks," said Stewart. "It was fun when you came onstage. And you weren't scared in front of the audience. Maybe we should do more plays now that you're over your stage fright. You're a good actor!"

"I am not," said Waldo. "Not as good as you."

"Yeah, well, I had fun, but I'm glad that's all over," said Stewart.

"You are?" said Sassy.

"Yeah, that was exhausting," said Stewart. "I'm glad to be getting back to our regular life."

"Do you love dogs?" asked Waldo.

"What kind of a question is that?" asked Stewart. "Of course I love dogs."

"Do you want to feed dogs sand for **dinner**?" asked Sassy.

"I would never do that," said Stewart.

"We did it!" said Waldo. "We saved Stewart!"

Waldo and Sassy wagged their tails.

"Are you ready for the cast party?" asked Stewart.

"Will there be a big pile of **food**?" asked Waldo. "We all know that the most exciting conclusion to a story is a big pile of **food**."

"Let's go find out," said Stewart.

They walked from the music room to their classroom. It was weird being in school at night, with dark classrooms and nearly empty hallways. When they opened the door to Ms. Twohey's room, it had been transformed into a fantastical wonderland beyond Waldo's and Sassy's imaginations.

There was, in fact, a very exciting conclusion. There was so much **food**. Spread over all the desks and table-tops were trays of **cookies**, **cupcakes**, and **vegetables**. There was a **bowl of punch** and three **Crock-Pots of chili**. There was a **watermelon** cut in the shape of Dogothy's basket and filled with **fruit**.

And **sandwiches**! So many **sandwiches**!

"I didn't know **sandwiches** could be so enormous," said Waldo in awe. "That **sandwich** is the size of six dachshunds lined up in a row."

"What I need you to do is drop that six-dachshund **sandwich** onto the floor so I can eat it," whispered Sassy.

"**Ralph! Ralph!**" said Waldo, clapping his paws together. "**You did a good job! It is okay that we did not get a lifetime supply of pizza, since you gave us a lifetime supply of many different kinds of food!**"

"Technically, our parents brought all this **food**," said Ralph, grabbing a **cookie**.

Waldo filled up two plates of **food**. He put one under a desk for Sassy and one on top of the desk for himself.

Stewart's dad came up to Salty. "I don't think we've met. I'm Stewart's dad."

"**Oh, hello**," said Waldo.

"You did a very good job as audio engineer, lighting coordinator, set manager, and surprise actor," said Stewart's dad.

"**I was just the button presser**," said Waldo, "**but thank you.**"

"And the Stewart saver," said Sassy quietly under the desk, her mouth full of sandwich.

"I had a fun time doing the play," Waldo told Stewart. "I got to press a bunch of buttons and make sounds and lights and wind. But the best part was the part at the end, where you went back to being Stewart."

"I was always going to be Stewart at the end, you know," said Stewart.

"Yes, because we were always going to save you," said Sassy. "Now someone get me another **sandwich**."

 **Julie Falatko** is the author of Snappsy the Alligator series, illustrated by Tim Miller; *No Boring Stories*, illustrated by Charles Santoso; and *The Great Indoors*, illustrated by Ruth Chan. Julie lives in Maine with her family, including her two dogs, and loves to make everyone (including the dogs) do skits in the living room. To learn more about Julie, please visit juliefalatko.com.

 **Colin Jack** is the illustrator of a number of books for children including *If You Happen to Have a Dinosaur*, *Under-the-Bed Fred*, *1 Zany Zoo*, and the Galaxy Zack series. He also works as a story artist and character designer in the animation industry and has been involved in the production of *Hotel Transylvania*, *The Book of Life*, *The Boss Baby*, and *Captain Underpants*: *The First Epic Movie*. Born in Vancouver, Colin currently resides in California with his wife and two sons.